THE SCAVENGERS RAISED THEIR RIFLES . . .

Blade's lightning reflexes were more than equal to the occasion. He simply slid the Commando's barrel over the lower rim of the window and squeezed the trigger. A torrent of slugs slammed into the leader's chest and smashed him into the fissure-ridden asphalt, geysers of blood spurting from his torso.

On the passenger side, Hickok leaned out the window and fired each Colt. Two of the men dropped, their craniums shattered.

The remaining pair were backpedaling frantically, shooting as they went, their shots deflected by the SEAL's impenetrable windshield.

Blade and Hickok ducked inside.

"What say we teach these cowchips a lesson?" Hickok asked.

Other books in the *Endworld* series:

ENDWORLD

#19:
CINCINNATI RUN
DAVID ROBBINS

LEISURE BOOKS ▮ NEW YORK CITY

Dedicated to . . .
Judy, Joshua, and Shane, for all the happiness.
And to the cherished memory of Aunt Evelyn and Uncle
Tyson.

A LEISURE BOOK®

January 1990

Published by

Dorchester Publishing Co., Inc.
276 Fifth Avenue
New York, NY 10001

Prologue

The copilot gazed out of the cockpit window at the thousands of people gathered near the terminal and gulped. "If we crash, I'll be so embarrassed."

"You won't be the only one," the captain muttered.

"I didn't realize President Toland planned to invite everyone in the Civilized Zone to witness our takeoff," the copilot said.

The captain laughed. "Sure looks like he did, doesn't it? There must be four thousand out there, but most are from Denver."

"What if we blow it, Skip?"

"We won't, Bob."

"I wish I had your confidence."

They both tensed as a voice crackled in their headsets.

"Captain Orton, this is your friendly controller in the tower speaking. Do you copy or are you peeing your pants?"

The captain grinned. "I copy, Max. What's up?"

"I just wanted to see if you're still awake," Max responded.

"We're raring to go," Captain Orton said.

"Between you and me, Skip, I wouldn't want to be in your shoes," Max commented.

"I wouldn't want you in my shoes either," Captain Orton quipped. "Your feet stink."

"Seriously, Skip. How's it going?"

"Everything checks out A-Okay," Captain Orton stated. "We've been through the preflight list twice, and all systems are go."

"President Toland is about to give his address to the crowd," Max mentioned. "Do you want me to pipe it into you guys?"

"Must we?" the copilot asked.

"Behave yourself, Bob," Captain Orton said. "We wouldn't be flying this bird if Toland hadn't pressed for the service. Let's hear what the man has to say."

"You're the boss," Bob replied, grinning.

"Let's hear the speech, Max," Captain Orton told the controller.

"You've got it," Max said.

A moment later their headsets hissed and sputtered, and the dulcet tones of President Toland reached their ears.

". . .for coming here today," the Chief Executive was saying. "This is truly a momentous occasion. Some might rightfully call this an historic occasion."

"I can see him," Bob remarked, craning his neck. "He's about twenty feet from our nose."

Captain Orton glanced down the nose of the 757 and spotted the familiar figure of the Civilized Zone's duly elected leader attired in a dark blue suit. "I see him too." President Toland's back was to the aircraft, but there was no mistaking those square shoulders or his neatly clipped black hair and his straight-as-an-arrow posture.

"And it is historic," Toland declared, talking into a microphone held in his right hand. "Think of it! This is the very first airline flight since World War Three, at least between members of the Freedom Federation. Once this flight has been successfully completed, we can expand our schedule to include other Federation members. California was selected this time because the L.A. Airport is fully operational." He paused for effect. "The word has gone out to the Flathead Indians in Montana, to the rugged frontiersmen and women who control the Dakota Territory, to the Moles in their underground city in northern Minnesota, to the Clan in northwestern Minnesota, and to the Family. They appreciate the importance of this flight. Restoring regular air service is but another rung on the ladder we must climb to return our respective societies to some semblance of our prewar greatness. . . ."

"Why do all politicians sound the same?" the copilot asked sarcastically.

"Hush," Captain Orton said.

"We have worked diligently and expended countless hours of hard effort, not to mention the cost in monetary terms, to rehabilitate the 757 you see behind me. We have salvaged parts from the aircraft abandoned in hangars here at Stapleton, and we have fabricated new parts where necessary. Two of our top officers, Captain Skip Orton and Lieutenant Bob Gunther, spent a year in California learning to fly the single-engine, twin-engine, and jet aircraft utilized by that sovereign State." He glanced over his right shoulder at the cockpit and smiled. "We can rest assured that our investment is in excellent hands."

"Then why are mine sweating?" Gunther quipped.

"Thanks for reminding me," Captain Orton responded.

"About what?" Lieutenant Gunther queried.

"I forgot to bring your diapers," Captain Orton said with a smile. "Maybe we can delay our takeoff while one of the stewardesses fetches extra towels."

"Anyone ever tell you that you have a nasty streak?" Gunther questioned.

"Sweet, innocent me?" Orton said.

They both shifted their attention to the President's speech.

". . .plans are already on the drawing board to expand our airline fleet to four airliners," Toland disclosed to his fidgety audience. "Within two years, if all goes well, we hope to establish weekly flights to each Federation faction. Fuel is our primary concern. California refines enough to barely meet its needs, and we produce a limited supply. Unfortunately, the days of our ancestors, the days of unlimited reserves of gas and oil, are long gone. Oh, it's not that the crude isn't out there, waiting to be brought to the surface. We know, for instance, that Wyoming alone could provide our needs for the immediate future, if we possessed more of the equipment needed to bring the crude to the surface. Our shortage of equipment and competent personnel is critical, and we hope to alleviate both in the next five years. . . ."

"He's putting me to sleep," Lieutenant Gunther remarked.

"He has a captive audience," Captain Orton commented. "We could be parked here an hour from now."

"But I can see that you're eager for the main event to begin," President Toland declared, and the crowd vented enthusiastic cheers. "But before I conclude, there's one crucial point which must be stressed."

"God deliver us from mutants, famine, and politicians," Lieutenant Gunther cracked.

"Amen," Captain Orton added.

"None of this would be possible without your cooperation. As citizens of the Civilized Zone, you have a right to feel proud of our achievement. The 757 would not get off the ground without your support."

"Without their tax dollars, he means," Gunther said.

"I should have brought a book," Orton observed.

". . .hold your heads up in more ways than one as this big bird takes to the air."

"Will that be this year?" someone in the throng shouted.

President Toland hesitated, surveying his restless constituents. "I can take a hint," he joked.

A ripple of laughter greeted his stab at humor.

"So let's get on with the show!" Toland stated, and walked toward the front of the assemblage, mingling with a row of other dignitaries; representatives from every Federation faction, members of Toland's administration, city officials from Denver and a dozen lesser municipalities, members of the media, and military bigwigs.

Orton and Gunther's headsets imitated frying bacon for several seconds.

"You heard the man, kiddies," Max the controller declared. "Time for the main event."

"What's the latest on the weather?" Captain Orton asked.

"Unlimited ceiling and unrestricted visibility," Max said. "The temperature is seventy-three. Just another gorgeous, sunny, September day in Colorado."

"Say, Max?" Lieutenant Gunther said.

"What, Bob?"

"Are you sure you know how to work the radar unit?"

Max snorted. "Are you maligning my professional integrity? I studied for eighteen months in California, and spent an entire year at the Los Angeles Airport. True, they don't have any birds this size flying out of L.A., but I learned everything there is to know about keeping track of your inept butts when you're in the air."

Gunther laughed and looked at Captain Orton. "I wonder if the air-traffic controllers in California are so sensitive?"

Orton was busy studying the instrument panel. "Let's get serious," he stated somberly. "We both know what's at stake on this flight. We've both flown the 757 on a dozen practice jaunts. Like Max, we've received the best training available. The Federation leaders consider this flight important for Federation morale. They see the airline service as a means of bringing the factions closer together. You heard President Toland." He paused and grinned. "Let's give the man his money's worth."

"Fine by me," Gunther said.

"Stapleton Tower, we're firing our engines," Captain Orton announced formally.

"Roger, Flight 1A," Max replied in kind. "You are cleared to use Taxiway Nine to Runway Eighteen."

"Thank you," Captain Orton said, and proceeded to start the engines.

A swell of excitement undulated through the crowd as the huge aircraft thundered to life, and many applauded. A collective, hearty shout arose when the jet lumbered slowly to the left and headed along Taxiway Nine.

Captain Orton looked at his copilot. "Flaps?"

"They're down," Lieutenant Gunther confirmed.

"We wouldn't want to make a basic blunder now," Captain Orton remarked.

"I wonder how our passengers are doing?" Gunther mentioned.

Captain Orton flicked a switch. "Ladies and gentlemen, this is your capain speaking. We will be taking off shortly. Please insure your seat belts are fastened. Once we are airborne, we will circle Stapleton Airport once, then climb to an elevation of twenty thousand feet. I will address you again when we're at cruising altitude. If you have any questions, just ask a stewardess. We hope you enjoy your trip, and trust you will fly Federation Airlines in the future." He clicked off.

"How many do we have on board, anyway?" Gunther inquired, scanning the array of instruments before him.

"Toland finally decided to allow forty to take the flight," Orton answered.

"Is that all?"

"I know we can carry almost four times that number, but forty passengers was all Toland would allow," Captain Orton said.

"And every passenger won their seat in the lottery?"

Orton nodded while scrutinizing Runway 18. "A lottery was the fairest method of picking the first passengers. Otherwise, only those with connections, the rich and the powerful, would get a seat."

The 757's engines whined as the aircraft rolled onto the runway.

"It's hard to believe this bird was built over one hundred and five years ago," Gunther commented.

"The 757's were put into service in the decade prior to the war," Captain Orton casually noted, checking the rudders.

"The airline industry was in a shambles, and the passenger traffic had fallen off drastically. So many of the aircraft were past their prime and on the verge of obsolescence that there were incidents where the jets simply fell apart in midair. Several major crashes were blamed on structural stress from old age. The cost of jet fuel was at a premium, and the larger birds, the 747's and such, became financially impractical to fly. The airlines were losing money hand over fist."

"An that's the reason they manufactured the 757's?"

"Yep. The 757's were the last of the new breed of aircraft, smaller, sleeker, and more fuel efficient. About fifty were put into service before the war."

"I hope this one holds together."

"Worrywart. The engineers and mechanics have gone over this bird with a fine-tooth comb. We've already flown fourteen hundred miles on our practice drills. She'll hold together," Captain Orton asserted.

"I'm ready when you are," Gunther said.

"Stapleton Tower, this is Federation Airlines Flight 1A. We are ready for takeoff," Orton announced.

Max responded immediately. "Flight 1A, you are cleared for takeoff on Runway 18. Happy flying."

Captain Orton directed the 757 into the wind and opened the throttle, grinning as the aircraft hurtled forward. In 15 seconds the wheels lifted gently off the smooth surface and the 757 climbed into the air. He retracted the landing gear and pulled up the flaps.

"All systems appear normal," Lieutenant Gunther stated.

The recently renovated buildings of Stapleton Airport appeared below them as they banked.

"You're on your way!" Max declared happily.

"Roger, Tower," Orton said smiling. He continued to ascend, executing a wide circle for the benefit of the passengers and the thousands on the ground now far below.

"I can't get over how small everything is from up here," Gunther observed. "The people look like ants."

Captain Orton grinned, starting to relax, his gaze on the

Rocky Mountains to the west, admiring the glistening, snow-capped peaks. "Beautiful," he murmured.

"What?"

"I'm glad I qualified for this post. Flying is the only job for me."

"Qualified?" Gunther said, and chuckled. "You tested out at the top of the applicants. No one is more qualified than you."

"You came in second by two points," Orton mentioned.

"Yeah," Gunther said. "I still think you cheated."

They both laughed, relieved to be up and away, anticipating the long flight to California with relish.

"Do you want me to buzz Gail for a coffee?" Gunther queried.

"Not yet," Captain Orton replied. He inspected the vertical-speed indicator and the altimeter. "What's the latest between you two anyway?"

"What are you talking about?"

"Are you going to ask her to marry you?"

Gunther glanced at the cockpit door. "Ssssh. She might walk in and hear you."

"So?"

"So she's been bugging me about marriage," Gunther revealed. "She wants a December wedding."

"And you don't?"

"I'm not ready for marriage," Gunther said.

"What are you waiting for? Old age?"

"You know me. I like playing the field. I'm not ready to settle down."

"You don't know what you're missing," Orton stated. "I've been married for nine years, and I've loved every minute of it."

"Even the four kids?"

"Especially the four kids."

Gunther shook his head. "I don't know how you do it."

"Do what?"

"Handle a big family. My younger brother has a wife and

two kids. Just two. If I go to visit for a week, they drive me up the wall. They yell and fight and spit and run all over the place. One of them even glued my shoes to the kitchen floor! I don't know how anyone can handle a family.''

''All children go through phases.''

''Maybe so. But I'm not ready for kids, and I'm certainly not ready for marriage. What's the rush? I have my whole life in front of me.''

Captain Orton gazed at the instrument panel. ''We're almost at twenty thousand feet.''

''Do you want me to take over?''

''Not yet, thanks. I like . . .'' Orton began, then stiffened.

A brilliant flash of crimson light enveloped the cockpit, casting the instrument panel in an eerie reddish glow.

''What the hell!'' Lieutenant Gunther blurted out.

Captain Orton could hear a muted, sizzling noise, and he reached up and tapped his headset.

''What's going on?'' Gunther asked, bewildered.

''I don't know,'' Orton admitted. The aircraft was still on course, steady and stable, but the sizzling was growing louder.

''What's that sound?'' Gunther inquired, gazing out the cockpit. ''Look! Even the nose is glowing red!''

Captain Orton started to angle the 757 in a tight turn.

''What are you doing?''

''Returning to Stapleton,'' Orton said. ''I don't like this.''

''What could it be?''

''Beats me,'' Orton said, frowning, alarmed by a dramatic increase in the bizarre sizzling.

''Is it me, or is the temperature rising?'' Gunther asked.

Captain Orton abruptly realized he was sweating profusely, and he looked at a circular gauge to his right. His breath caught in his throat. ''The temperature *is* climbing! It's ninety in here!''

''It can't be the engines,'' Gunther said.

The cockpit door unexpectedly opened, and in dashed a lovely brunette in a prim blue uniform. ''The passengers are scared to death. What's happening?''

Gunther twisted in his seat. "We don't know, Gail. Try and keep them calm."

"It's so hot," she declared.

"We're returning to Stapleton," Captain Orton said. "Advise the passengers."

"Will do," Gail responded, and turned toward the door. She never made it.

The red radiance intensified, attaining the shimmering luster of a miniature sun, while simultaneously the temperature soared, the heat blistering the occupants of the cockpit.

"Damn!" Lieutenant Gunther exclaimed. "I can hardly breathe!"

Captain Orton gasped as a violent vibration shook the aircraft, and he struggled to maintain control, but the 757 started to dive of its own accord.

Gail screamed.

A moment later the azure sky above Stapleton Airport was rent by an explosion of tremendous magnitude.

Chapter One

The giant gaped at the billowing fireball, aghast. His brawny hands clenched at his sides, his knobby knuckles protruding. "Dear Spirit, no!" he blurted out, horrified to his core.

"What the blazes happened?" asked a lean man in buckskins standing to the giant's right.

"Did you see that strange red light?" asked the stocky Indian in green on the giant's left.

"I saw it," the giant confirmed, his penetrating gray eyes locked on the roiling, flaring cloud to the west of the airport. A comma of dark hair hung over his right brow. His features were ruggedly handsome, his physique outstanding. Every muscle on his seven-foot frame bulged, developed to perfection by years of vigorous exercise. A black leather vest covered his huge chest. Green fatigue pants and black combat boots completed his attire. Resting on each hip was a large Bowie knife, snug in its sheath.

"What the blazes happened, Blade?" the man in the buckskins repeated in a daze. His hair was blond, as was his sweeping mustache. Eyes the color of a crystal-clear mountain lake were wide in disbelief. Strapped around his narrow waist were a pair of pearl-handled Colt Python revolvers.

"I don't know, Hickok," the giant called Blade answered. "I just don't know."

"That light had something to do with the explosion," the Indian said. "I just know it." He was powerfully built, his black hair stirring in the breeze, his brown eyes squinting upward, his body clothed in a green shirt and pants constructed from a section of canvas tent. Both the Indian and the gunman wore moccasins.

"For once, Geronimo, I've got to agree with you," Hickok said.

"If you think I'm right, then I must be wrong," Geronimo responded, absently placing his right hand on the tomahawk angled under his black belt over his right hip.

"Smart-alecky Injun," Hickok mumbled.

"Can it, you two," Blade ordered, glancing at the throng to their rear. Not a word was being spoken. The audience was deathly still, staring skyward at the subsiding fireball.

"This is a tragic calamity," declared the elderly man in front of the giant. "Intentionally performed, I'd say."

Blade swiveled and thoughtfully regarded his aged mentor. "Should we call for an emergency Council of the Federation leaders, Plato?"

Plato shook his head, his long gray beard swaying with the motion. He was in his fifties, and the experience of his years was etched in the deep wrinkles lining his visage. His blue eyes were alert and bright, belying his seemingly frail constitution. Faded, patched jeans and a brown wool shirt hung loosely on his body. "No," he said. "Calling for an emergency Council would necessitate awaiting the arrival of those leaders currently not present. We would waste precious time."

"But four of the leaders are here," Blade noted.

"And the rest have sent representatives," Plato said. "So we should convene an emergency session of those leaders and representatives on hand. The absent leaders will understand, once they are apprised of the gravity of the situation."

Blade nodded. As usual, the Family's sagacious leader had shown incontrovertible logic. He looked to the right at the row of dignitaries.

Just beyond Hickok stood President Toland, his countenance conveying his intense inner torment. The head of the Civilized Zone, one of the two key figures instrumental in bringing the concept of a Federation Airline to fruition, the man who had diligently directed the renovation of the 757 and the rehabilitation of Stapleton Airport, was devastated. Tears welled in his blue eyes. "Dear Lord, no!" he exclaimed.

Plato walked up to the president and draped his right hand on Toland's left shoulder. "Nick, we must disperse the crowd."

Toland said nothing, his mouth slack, a tear streaking his left cheek.

"Nick, are you okay?" Plato queried.

"Forty-five people are dead!" President Toland said. "And it's all my fault."

Plato's shoulders slumped. "The destruction of the 757 wasn't your fault. You know that."

"My fault," President Toland stated, gazing into Plato's kindly eyes.

"Snap out of it," Plato said. "Your people need you. We must disperse the crowd and attend to business."

President Toland straightened at the mention of the gathering, taking a deep breath and wiping his left hand across his cheek. "Sorry. You're right. Thanks." He turned and surveyed the sea of pale faces.

"I don't envy him," Geronimo said softly to Hickok.

"The measure of a man is the grit he shows when the chips are down," the gunman remarked in a whisper.

Geronimo did a double take. "Since when did you become a philosopher?"

"I'm no slouch in the smarts department. Ask anybody. They'll tell you that I'm full of bright ideas."

"You're full of something, all right, but it's brown and

keeps seeping out of your ears.''

President Toland raised his arms aloft. ''My fellow citizens, hear me! I know that many of you are still in shock. I know that many of you had relatives on Flight 1A, and I share your grief. You all saw what happened. What we don't know is why. I'm about to get to the bottom of this catastrophe, and I need your help.''

The crowd began to stir sluggishly.

''Stapleton Airport will be closed until further notice,'' Toland announced. ''The military will seal off the airport in fifteen minutes. Only those directly related to the victims on the 757 will be permitted to remain in the terminal. Please. We must seal off the area. Kindly leave now. Your cooperation in this matter will be greatly appreciated.'' He swung to his left, looking at a lean man in a neat military uniform sporting gold insignia on the shoulders. ''General Reese, have your men expedite the evacuation. I want all nonessential personnel removed promptly.''

General Reese saluted. ''Consider it done,'' he said, and stalked off.

''I want to call an immediate meeting of the Federation leaders and representatives present,'' Plato said to Toland. ''Where can we conduct our session in private?''

President Toland glanced at the terminal. ''There's a room on the second floor ideal for our purposes.''

''Excellent. Would you relay the word to the others?''

''Of course. Since I must bear the burden of responsibility for the flight, and since Denver is my capital, I'll chair the meeting unless you would rather have the chore.''

''The honor is all yours,'' Plato said.

Toland snorted. ''Some honor. The innocent blood of forty-five people is on my hands.''

''You exaggerate, dear friend.''

''Do I? We'll see if you change your mind later,'' President Toland said. ''Should we start the meeting in five minutes?''

''The sooner, the better,'' Plato said. ''The Warriors and I will proceed on ahead.''

"Be my guest. Take the south stairs to the second floor, and you'll find the room you want behind the third door on the right."

"We'll meet you there," Plato stated.

President Toland hurried along the row of VIP's.

"What did he mean about changing your mind?" Blade asked Plato.

The head of the Family pursed his thin lips. "Perhaps he has pertinent information to reveal," he speculated.

"Let's mosey to the meetin' room," Hickok suggested.

"What's your rush?" Geronimo wanted to know.

"I need to tinkle."

Geronimo made a show of surveying the area. "Looks like you'll have to hold it in."

"Why?"

"There isn't a tree in sight."

Plato was staring at the throng. "Perhaps five minutes is not enough time. How will we ever get through this crowd?"

"Allow me," Blade said, and forged into the assemblage. "Excuse us!" he declared in his deep voice. Those in front of the Warrior glanced at him and quickly parted to permit his passage.

Plato, Hickok, and Geronimo followed.

"It's like I've always said, pard," Hickok mentioned to Geronimo. "Never argue with a mutant, an angry buffalo, and a guy seven feet tall."

"I've never heard you say that."

"Well, actually, I just made it up."

"Do tell."

"Why the dickens are you pickin' on me, anyway?" Hickok inquired.

"I'm a sucker for an easy mark," Geronimo said.

"Are you insulting my intelligence again?"

"I'd never belabor the obvious."

"What?"

"Forget it."

"What's a woman havin' a baby got to do with this?"

Geromino smirked. "Just forget it, will you?"

Plato looked over his left shoulder at the pair of bickering Warriors. "Gentlemen," he said sternly.

"What'd we do now?' Hickok queried.

"I know you are trained to adjust readily to adversity, to take misfortune in stride," Plato commented. "I know the Warriors are trained to employ humor to relieve stress—"

"Yeah? So?" Hickok interrupted.

"This is definitely not the time or place," Plato observed harshly.

Hickok and Geronimo gazed around them at the slowly dispersing audience, most of whom were emotionally ravaged by the explosion. Morosely, conversing in subdued tones, many sniffling and dabbing at their eyes, the people were shuffling toward the terminal, through which they would have to pass to reach the parking lots beyond.

"Sorry, old-timer," Hickok said.

Blade glanced back at the gunman and glared.

"Sensitivity, Nathan, is a trait even Warriors should cultivate," Plato advised Hickok.

"A Warrior can't afford to be too mushy," Hickok responded.

"Mushy?"

"We go up against mutants or lowlifes at least once a month," Hickok mentioned. "We've got to be on our toes every minute of the day, and we've got to be ready to shoot first and ask questions later. If Warriors get too sensitive, they start lettin' their emotions get in the way of their better judgment. And when that happens, they're as good as dead."

"I'm fully aware of the psychology of being a proper Warrior," Plato said. "The Founder created the Warrior class to protect the Home and safeguard the Family. He intended the Warriors to be superbly efficient fighters, to be the best at their craft. But he never intended the Warriors to forsake all emotion in order to function effectively. Do you remember your Schooling years?"

"Of course."

"And what was the paramount teaching of the Elders?" Hickok sighed.

"What was it?" Plato prodded, staying on Blade's heels as the giant continued to press toward the terminal.

"To love the Spirit and our brothers and sisters on this planet," Hickok answered in a restrained tone.

"Have you forgotten the supreme teaching?"

"Nope. Just amended it."

"In what manner?" Plato asked.

"I'm all for lovin' other folks," Hickok explained. "This old world would be a heap better off if everyone really did try to live the supreme teaching, but everyone doesn't. There are a lot of nasty types runnin' around, ready to blow your head off for no reason at all. Look at what just happened to that jet." He paused and frowned. "As a Warrior, I can't go waltzin' around with a smile on my puss and love in my heart like Joshua does all the time—"

"Joshua is our Family's spiritual counselor," Plato interjected. "He has realized the living of the supreme teaching in his life."

"Yeah, but Josh doesn't go around killin' mangy varmints for a livin'. I do. It's my job to make sure no one harms any of our Family, and I'll admit I've plugged my fair shair of cow-chips. I know we all pass on to the higher mansions sooner or later, but I don't much cotton to the notion of being sent there before my time by some wacko. I have a missus and a young'un I'm rather fond of, and I intend to spend the next twenty or thirty years with them. So I tend to keep a tight rein on my emotions, except around my loved ones. I try to give everyone else the benefit of the doubt, to treat them as my spiritual brothers and sisters, unless, of course, they look at me crossways."

"And then?"

"I shoot 'em in the head."

Plato stared at the gunfighter. "One of these days we must discuss your outlook on life."

"Is there something wrong with it?" Hickok asked.

"Not at all," Plato said. "Your attitude is ideal for a Warrior. But I must confess that I'm troubled by your lack of remorse over the lives you've taken."

"Give me a break. Do you expect us to get all misty-eyed every time we blow away a scavenger or a raider?"

"Don't you feel any compassion for the enemies you've slain?"

"Heaps of it," Hickok assured the Family leader. "Why do you think I shoot the coyotes in the head? I don't want them to suffer."

"I was under the impression that you shoot your foes in the head because a shot through the brain is more likely than any other to instantaneously slay the . . .cow-chips."

"Well, that too," Hickok admitted.

Plato smiled. "Nathan, you're a pip."

The Warriors and the Family's leader reached a point 20 feet from the terminal doors.

"Where are Toland and the others?" Hickok inquired, surveying the throng to their rear.

"They'll catch up," Geronimo said.

Plato abruptly halted, turning to gaze at the lingering vestige of the fireball. "Most extraordinary," he commented.

"What is?" Geronimo queried.

"Did you observe any debris descending to the ground?"

"No," Geronimo said. "But the 757 was bearing to the west. The debris may have fallen into the center of Denver."

"Did you see any fall?"

"No."

"Most extraordinary." Plato repeated, and walked after Blade.

"What was that all about?" Hickok asked.

"Beats me," Geronimo said.

"If you ask me, the man needs to eat more veggies."

"Why?" Geronimo questioned.

"My mon always told me to eat my veggies or my mind would wind up warped," the gunman elaborated.

"That explains everything."

Chapter Two

"You won't like what you're about to hear," President Toland predicted.

"Allow us to judge for ourselves," Plato suggested, surveying the occupants of the room.

Eleven people were gathered in the conference chamber on the second floor of the Stapleton Terminal. Four stood near the closed door: Blade, Hickok, Geronimo, and General Reese. Seated at the rectangular wooden table were four Federation leaders and three representatives. President Toland sat at the head of the table, his back to a window affording a magnificent view of the imposing Rockies.

To Toland's right was the frontiersman called Kilrane, a strapping man in the typical postwar garb of his people, buckskins. Kilrane was the head of the Calvary, the fiercely independent horde of horsemen who ruled the Dakota Territory. His hair was a light brown tinged with gray streaks, his eyes a deep blue. A Mitchell single-action revolver filled a holster on his right hip.

Sitting on Kilrane's right was the leader of the Clan, a handsome man named Zahner. Originally his followers had resided in the gloomy, desolate shambles of the Twin Cities. Zahner had led one of three gangs struggling to survive in Minneapolis and St. Paul, until several Warriors and Joshua had arrived in the former metropolis. Joshua had persuaded the gangs to cease their hostilities, and the Family had aided them in relocating in the small town of Halma located in northwestern Minnesota. Zahner wore black trousers and a faded white shirt.

Next to Zahner was a jovial, rotund character wearing brown pants and a yellow shirt. His name was Crofton, and he was the official representative for the Federation faction known as the Moles. Prior to the war, a group of survivalists had excavated an underground complex in north-central Minnesota. Their descendants later expanded the complex into a sprawling subterranean city that was currently ruled with an iron fist by an egotistical man called Wolfe. Wolfe seldom attended Federation functions, and Crofton served as his eyes and ears.

After Crofton came White Eagle, the delegate from the Flathead Indians, the tribe controlling the former state of Montana. Their leader was a lovely woman called Star. The entire tribe had voted on White Eagle's selection as their standby representative. His responsibility was to stand in for Star whenever she was unable to meet her obligations. A bout with the flu had prevented her from being present in Denver for the inaugural flight of the 757. White Eagle wore beaded buckskins and an elaborate headdress.

Seated beside Plato was the California delegate, a woman named Eudora Macquarie. She functioned as the Undersecretary of State, and her presence was directly attributable to her lowly status in the administration of Governor Melnick. Unlike the Civilized Zone, which consisted of the former states of Nebraska, Kansas, Wyoming, Colorado, Oklahoma, New Mexico, the northern half of Texas, and portions of Arizona, and was the successor of the once-mighty United States of America, the state of California still referred to its Chief Executive as a governor and not a president. Because Governor Melnick was one of the prime architects of the Federation Airline concept, along with President Toland, and because Melnick and his top staff, most of whom were professional politicians, wanted to be on hand to receive the praise and admiration of their constituents when the 757 arrived in L.A., Melnick had sent Eudora Macquarie to fill in on the Denver end. A prim woman wearing a full-length beige dress, she now sat with her arms folded on the table and her green eyes on President Toland.

"I want you to know that I accept full responsibility for the loss of the 757 and the people on board," the Civilized Zone's leader was saying. "I should have postponed the flight until the information I recently received was verified."

"What information?" Kilrane inquired.

"Spit it out, man," Crofton said.

Toland rested his elbows on the table and held his head in his hands, the picture of misery. "I should start at the beginning," he stated, and looked at Plato. "Was it in July that one of the Hurricanes disappeared?"

Plato was surprised by the query. "Yes," he confirmed. "The VTOL had transported Blade and two other Warriors to Florida, but it never returned to retrieve them."

Toland nodded. "Okay. As I'm sure all of you are aware, California owns a pair of technological marvels, two jets with vertical-takeoff-and-landing capability. VTOLs they're called, and they're utilized as shuttles between the Federation factions and to ferry strike teams to hot spots. In July one of the jets took Blade to a spot near Miami. We know the Hurricane returned to California after being refueled by a tanker en route. The pilot, a Captain Lyle Stuart, was sent to pick up Blade and the other Warriors a week later." He paused, frowning.

"The Hurricane never arrived," Blade said, finishing for him. "My friends and I were forced to return to the Home through the Outlands."

The leaders and representatives exchanged knowing glances.

They were all familiar with the dreaded Outlands, the designation applied to all areas existing outside the few organized territories. The Russians governed a belt of land in the eastern half of the country, and in the wake of World War Three over a dozen strong city-states had arisen, each under the thumb of a different group or leader. But the Russians, the city-states, and the Federation members were the exception, not the rule. Most of the once-proud United States of America had reverted to a primitive state of savagery, where the survival of the fittest was the acknowledged law of the land.

"How long did it take you to get back to your Home from Miami?" Crofton queried.

"Three months," Blade answered.

"And the trip was sheer hell every step of the way," Zahner commented. He had previously discussed the journey with Blade.

"It wasn't easy," the head Warrior stated.

"I thought it was a piece of cake," Hickok quipped.

"Were you with Blade?" Kilrane asked.

"Yep," the gunman said.

"Now you know why it took three months," Geronimo remarked.

Blade gazed at President Toland. "We never did discover the reason the Hurricane failed to return."

"I may know," Toland said sadly.

"No one told us," Plato mentioned.

"I haven't told anyone," President Toland responded. "And I committed a terrible blunder."

"We're listening," Plato stated.

Toland sat back in his chair. "Five days ago I stumbled across information concerning the missing jet. I should explain. The Civilized Zone is the largest Federation faction. Our borders are widespread, and we must continually patrol our boundaries for mutants, raiders, and scavengers." He rubbed his chin slowly, his lips compressing. "We also keep a watch out for black marketeers who are attempting to smuggle contraband into the Civilized Zone. All of you know about the black market. Because of the chronic shortages we all face, the black market flourishes. None of us have much of a manufacturing capability. To tell you the truth, I don't much mind having food, clothing, and other necessities smuggled in, but I draw the line at drugs, alcohol, and less savory products. Six days ago one of our border patrols apprehended a smuggler trying to bring cocaine in. We had him dead to rights, and he knew it.''

"He offered to make a deal," Blade guessed.

"Exactly," President Toland said. "He claimed he possessed information vital to the Federation's future. The interrogating officer didn't believe him for a minute, not until the smuggler alleged he knew the whereabouts of a Federation jet.''

Blade took a stride toward the table. "He knew about the missing Hurricane?"

"The smuggler claimed he'd been in Russian territory several weeks ago, and while he was there he'd heard an interesting story. There was a rumor going around that the Reds had shot down a Federation jet and retrieved it,'' Toland said.

"How?" Blade inquired. "The Russians don't have any functional fighters left, and the VTOLs fly at a high altitude when passing over the Russian region, too high for the Soviets to employ anti-aircraft weaponry.''

Toland scowled in self-reproach. "Here's the rub. The smuggler told us the Russians have developed a new weapon, a means of downing an aircraft at any altitude and at any range.''

"And you think the Russians used the same weapon on the 757?" Eudora Macquarie interjected.

"Possibly," Toland said.

"What type of weapon is it?" Eudora questioned.

"We have no idea."

"When was it constructed?" she pressed him.

"We don't know if it really was," Toland replied, then

corrected himself. "At least we didn't, until today."

"A new Soviet weapon would account for the peculiar explosion we witnessed," Plato commented, and suddenly he was the focus of every eye in the room. He deliberated for a minute before continuing, well aware of the influence he brought to bear at Federation Council meetings. Although the Family was the smallest Federation faction numerically and geographically, with approximately a hundred Family members residing in a walled 30-acre compound, the Family Elders, and especially Plato, were widely respected for their wisdom. When Plato spoke, the other Federation leaders listened attentively. "Every system on the 757 was tested repeatedly before today's takeoff. Practice flights were conducted to insure the aircraft was airworthy. There was no logical reason for the airliner to explode, and yet it did." He scratched at his beard.

"An engine malfunction could account for the explosion," Eudora noted.

"True" Plato agreed, "except for a few disturbing details. An engine malfunction would not account for the red light we saw. I'm positive a streak of crimson light struck the 757 shortly before the blast."

"All of us saw the red light," Kilrane said.

"There was another unusual aspect to the explosion," Plato informed them. "There wasn't any debris."

"Debris?" White Eagle repeated, puzzled.

"If an engine had malfunctioned and the aircraft simply blew up, then there should have been debris. Pieces of the jet should have fallen to earth in the city," Plato detailed, and looked at General Reese. "Have you received any reports of falling parts yet?"

"None," General Reese replied. "No wings, no fuselage, no bodies, nothing."

"I don't understand," Crofton said. "Where did the bits and pieces go?"

"Therein lies the key to this mystery," Plato stated. "There should have been debris. Gravity will not be denied. Since there wasn't any debris, then the 757 must have been totally obliterated *in the air.*"

"No known weapon could do that," Zahner declared. "No explosion either."

"True," Plato concurred. "Which indicates we witnessed an *implosion,* not an explosion."

"What the hell is the difference?" Crofton queried.

"There's a great deal of difference," Plato elaborated. "An explosion is a violent expansion of an object invariably produced by a chemical agent or a mechanical means. An implosion, however, is the opposite. An implosion occurs when an object bursts inward."

"I don't get it," Crofton said.

"Have you ever eaten an orange?" Plato asked him.

The Mole blinked a few times. "Yeah. So?"

"What would happen if you threw an orange against a boulder? Would the fruit explode?"

"Yeah," Crofton replied.

"But if you held the orange in your hand and made a fist, what would happen?"

"I'd crush it."

"Precisely my point. The force applied by your hand would cause the orange to turn inward upon itself. This is a crude illustration, granted. But perhaps, just perhaps, an external force was applied to the 757, a force that caused the aircraft to burst inward, a force that created an implosion and simultaneously consumed every particle of the airliner."

"The red light?" Kilrane questioned.

"That would be my conclusion," Plato said. "The red light completely enveloped the aircraft, even while the implosion was transpiring. I believe the 757 and the bodies of those poor people were somehow reduced to mere dust."

"What kind of weapon could do such a thing?" Zahner asked.

"I lack sufficient data to extrapolate," Plato responded.

"Which brings us back to square one," Eudora Macquarie said. "We suspect the Russians have developed a new weapon, but we don't have concrete evidence supporting our suspicion. We don't know what type of weapon it is, and we don't know where this weapon is based, whether it's mobile or stationary.''

President Toland cleared his throat. ''I might be able to help there.''

Everyone turned toward the head of the table.

''The smuggler claimed he'd heard through the black-market grapevine that the Reds have based this weapon at a military facility in Ohio,'' Toland disclosed.

''Did he supply the name of this facility?'' Eudora inquired.

Toland shook his head. ''No, but he did give us the name of the city where the facility is supposedly located.''

''Which city?'' Zahner probed.

''Cincinnati.''

The leaders and delegates shifted in their seats and eyed one another, their features registering skepticism.

''Are you trying to tell us that a 757 flying over Denver was shot down by a weapon based in Cincinnati, Ohio?'' Kilrane said, voicing the thought uppermost on their minds.

President Toland shrugged. ''I can only relay the information we received from the smuggler. But now you can appreciate why we didn't believe him, why I decided to hold the inaugural flight as scheduled.'' His head drooped, his mouth curling downward. ''If I'd only given him the benefit of the doubt.''

''Maybe the lousy commies have come up with a new weapon,'' Crofton said. ''But there's no way in hell they can shoot a plane down from hundreds of miles away.'' He paused and looked at Plato. ''Is there?''

Plato was deep in contemplation, absently chewing on his lower lip. He roused himself and gazed at the Mole. ''Possibly. I've read a number of books in the Family library dealing with the prewar technology. Their accomplishments were astounding. There were trains capable of traveling over one hundred miles an hour. There were boats that rode over the water on cushions of air. And we've all heard the stories about the space flights, about the trips made to the moon and Mars.''

Crofton snickered. "Yeah. We've all heard the tales about the good old days, when men and women could do anything. It's all a crock."

"You don't believe our ancestors traveled to other planets?" Plato queried.

"No way, man," Crofton said.

"Why not, may I ask?"

"If I haven't seen something with my own eyes, I find it hard to believe," Crofton explained.

"But we all saw the 757 destroyed," Plato noted.

There was a moment of silence.

"Okay," Zahner said. "Let's assume the Russians have a new weapon. Let's assume the smuggler told the truth. What are we going to do about it?"

"There is only one recourse," Plato stated, and glanced at the three Warriors. "We must send someone to Cincinnati to investigate."

Hickok glanced at Blade. "Why is he lookin' at us?"

"Three guesses," the giant replied, then walked to the edge of the table. "Do you want us to go?"

"The decision must be yours," Plato said.

Blade looked at his fellow Warriors. The three of them comprised one of the six Triads into which the Warrior class was divided. Alpha Triad was their code name, and together they had journeyed far and wide to counter threats against the Family and the Freedom Federation. As the head of the Alpha Triad, and as the commander of all the Warriors, Blade would make the ultimate decision. But like him, Hickok and Geronimo both had families. He felt constrained to offer them the opportunity to decline. As the top Warrior, such a luxury was denied him. "What will it be?" he asked them. "Do you want to go?"

"We have a choice?" Hickok answered in surprise. "Well, in that case, I'll pass. My missus will clobber me if I don't get back on time. She hates to do the dishes by herself."

"I'll go," Geronimo volunteered.

"That makes two of us," Blade said reluctantly.

Hickok looked from one to the other. "Thanks a lot, you ding-a-lings. If you're going, I'm going."

"You don't have to go," Blade offered.

"Where you guys go, I go," the gunman declared, then smirked. "Besides, someone has to baby-sit you yahoos."

"Lucky us," Geronimo said.

"Then it's settled," Blade stated. "Alpha Triad will head for Cincinnati." He glanced at Plato. "When do you want us to leave?"

"I will remain in Denver while you are gone," Plato said. "Time is of the essence. The Soviet weapon must be located and neutralized expeditiously. We would waste precious time if you transported me to the Home prior to your departure. The other Elders will supervise our Family in my absence." He gazed at each of the Warriors fondly.

"So you want us to leave *now,* old-timer?" Hickok asked.

Plato grinned. "My compliments on your intellect."

The gunfighter looked at Geronimo and beamed. "See? What did I tell you?"

Chapter Three

"I don't like the looks of this, pard."

"You and me, both," Blade agreed, his hands tightening on the steering wheel.

"Do we go around them?" Geronimo asked.

"No," Blade said. "We can use some fresh meat. If they try anything, waste them."

Hickok chuckled. "Now you're talkin' my language."

Blade removed his right foot from the brake and eased down on the accelerator. The SEAL's engine purred as the vehicle headed toward the cluster of tents and shacks situated at the base of the low hill.

"I'm glad the Founder had his engineers make this buggy bulletproof," Hickok said. "If the jokers down there start something, they're in for the shock of their lives."

Blade nodded. The Family's Founder, as he was called, a wealthy survivalist named Kurt Carpenter, had expended millions of dollars to have the SEAL developed. The Solar Energized Amphibious or Land Recreational Vehicle was a prototype, the first of its kind, and thanks to the war the *only* one of its kind. In appearance the SEAL resembled a van, with its boxlike body composed of a shatterproof and heat-resistant plastic, tinted green to enable those within to see out but preventing anyone outside from observing the interior. The floor was an impervious metal alloy, while four enormous, puncture-resistant tires, each two feet wide and four feet high, supported the transport.

The SEAL received its power from the sun. Sunlight was collected by a pair of solar panels attached to the roof, then converted and stored in unique, revolutionary batteries located in a lead-lined case under the vehicle. The scientists had guaranteed Carpenter the SEAL would function indefinitely provided the battery casings and the solar panels were not damaged.

While he had been pleased with the SEAL's capabilities, Carpenter had not been satisfied; he knew his descendants would need more than an all-terrain vehicle to endure in a world ravaged by a nuclear holocaust. Consequently, after the automotive geniuses were finished with the development stage, he took the transport to another group of experts, men and women whose stock in trade was killing. He hired mercenaries to outfit the SEAL with armaments, and he received his money's worth.

The SEAL was a virtual arsenal on wheels. A pair of 50-caliber machine guns were mounted underneath each front headlight. A flamethrower was positioned behind the front fender. There was a rocket-launcher in the center of the front grill. And there was a miniature surface-to-air missile concealed in the roof above the driver's seat. The weapons were activated by silver toggle switches on the dashboard. A simple flick of a toggle, and the appropriate armament would slide out from its hidden housing and commence firing.

"We shouldn't get trigger-happy," Geronimo cautioned. "These people might be friendly."

"We'll soon know," Blade said, glancing around. "But be ready, just in case."

The interior of the SEAL was roomy. There were two bucket seats in the front separated by a console. Hickok was sitting in the passenger seat. Behind the bucket seats was a wide seat, in which Geronimo sat, and the rear third of the vehicle was used as a storage section for their spare ammunition, food and other provisions.

"I'm ready," Geronimo assured the giant. He wore an Arminius .357 Magnum in a shoulder holster under his left arm, in addition to the tomahawk under his belt. Resting on his lap was a Springfield Armory SAR, converted to full automatic by the Family Gunsmiths.

"So am I," Hickok said eagerly. He held a Colt AR-15 in his right hand.

Blade looked down at the Commando Arms Carbine on the console to his right. The 45-caliber Commando, with its 90-shot magazine, resembled the ancient Thompson-style submachine gun and was his favorite firearm.

"A short stop won't hurt us," Geronimo commented. "We've been making good time."

"We're almost to Red Territory, aren't we?" Hickok inquired.

Geronimo picked up a map from the seat beside him. "We're west of Watseka, Illinois. I estimate we're about eighty or ninety miles north of the Russian lines."

"You *estimate?*" Hickok repeated.

"It's not like I have a map of the Soviet territory," Geronimo responded. "We know the Russians control most of New England, southern New York, southern Pennsylvania, New Jersey, Maryland, Kentucky, Virginia, and West Virginia. We also know they have sections of North and South Carolina, as well as southern Ohio, southern Indiana, and parts of Illinois under their thumb. But we don't know the exact boundaries."

"How far are we from the Home?" the gunman questioned.

"I haven't calculated the miles to Lake Bronson State Park," Geronimo replied, referring to the former scenic area in northwestern Minnesota near which the Home was located.

"Why?"

"I was just thinkin' of Sherry and my little buckaroo, Ringo," Hickok mentioned.

"I miss Cynthia and Cochise," Geronimo addmitted.

"What about you, pard?" Hickok questioned Blade.

"Need you ask?" the giant responded.

"Sorry. I know you miss Jenny and Gabe as much as we miss our kin," Hickok said.

"Once, just once, I wish you'd talk like everyone else," Geronimo declared.

"What's wrong with the way I talk?" Hickok demanded.

"As I've told you a million times, you sound like an idiot."

"Takes one to know one."

Geromino leaned forward. "For years you've been talking like you think the real Wild Bill Hickok talked. I know Hickok was your childhood hero. I know you admired the man so much that you took his name at your Naming ceremony. But you're going overboard. Do you hear me talking like the Geronimo of old?"

"No."

"Does Sundance talk like the Sundance Kid?"

"No."

"Does Samson use bibilical language?"

"No."

"Does Teucer speak Greek?"

"No."

"And what about Plato?"

"What about him?" Hickok retorted. "He uses so many blamed highfalutin words, I never know what in Sam Hill he's talkin' about."

"Okay. Forget Plato. But you get my point. All of us went through the Naming ceremony instituted by the Founder. All of us had the option of researching the history books in the library the Founder stocked and picking the name of any historical figure as our own. We can take our name from other sources, if we wish—"

"Tell me something I don't know," Hickok quipped.

Geronimo ignored the dig. "The Founder initiated the Naming ceremony as a way of insuring we never lose sight of our historical roots. He didn't intend for us to completely copy our heroes in every respect."

"Are you referrin' to me?"

"Who else is a living dictionary of the Wild West?"

"Is that what I am?" Hickok asked, and smiled. "Gee. I'm flattered."

"Boys," Blade stated with special emphasis, interrupting their banter. "We're expected."

Hickok and Geronimo faced front.

The SEAL was still 500 yards from the tents and shacks. There appeared to be about a dozen of each, lined in uneven rows on both sides of the cracked, pitted, pothole-dotted highway. They passed a faded, rusted sign indicating the road was once known as Highway 24.

"Look at 'em all," Hickok said.

Over three dozen men, women, and children were milling about the encampment. Most wore tattered clothing. Many of the men and women carried weapons, either a rifle, a revolver, or both. Five men were standing in the roadway, strung out across Highway 24, watching the transport apporach. All five held rifles.

"Are they the welcoming committee?" Geronimo queried.

"Looks that way," Blade said.

"Let me talk to them," Hickok proposed.

"I'll do the talking," Blade replied.

"Why you?"

"For two reasons," Blade answered. "One, you're likely to gun them down before we find out what they want."

"And what's the second reason?"

Blade glanced at the gunman. "I said so."

Hickok shrugged. "You're the head honcho."

"They look like scavengers," Geronimo commented, "but scavengers never stay in one place."

"Maybe they're startin' their own town," Hickok speculated.

"In the middle of nowhere?" Geronimo said.

"Some folks have no common sense, pard."

Geronimo gave the gunman a meaningful look. "Don't I know it."

Blade applied the brakes lightly when the SEAL was 40 yards from the five men. He allowed the transport to glide forward slowly, his eyes on the quintet of hardcases. A glint of sunlight off to the right arrested his attention, and he saw several antiquated vehicles parked in a stand of trees to the south of the tents and shacks. The afternoon sun was gleaming off the front bumper of a white car. Although the bumper and grill were visible, the car's body was obscured by dense brush. For that matter, all of the vehicles were partially screened by undergrowth. Blade's eyes narrowed.

Wait a minute.

Were those vehicles parked in the trees—or *hidden* there?

"Everyone is lookin' at us," Hickok observed.

All of the people in the camp had ceased whatever they were doing and were staring at the SEAL.

"This setup is definitely a trap," Blade announced. "We'll let them make the first move." He rolled down his window.

Hickok was doing the same. He placed the AR-15 between his legs, drew his Pythons, and held the revolvers next to the passenger-side door, just below the edge of the window.

The transport was now ten yards from the bedraggled men, none of whom displayed the slightest inclination to move aside.

Blade brought the SEAL to a stop six feet away and poked his head out the window. "Hello," he said with a smile.

"Hi, stranger," declared the man in the middle, a hefty fellow with a cleft chin and bushy brows. He wore a torn flannel shirt and baggy brown pants, and in his hands was a Winchester 30-30. "Nice van you have here. Never saw one like it before."

"It's special," Blade said.

"Is that so?" Hefty responded, smiling in a friendly fashion. "Would you happen to have fresh venison you'd be willing to trade?'' Blade inquired politely. ''We've been eating jerky for the past two days and could use a change.''

Hefty nodded and came around the front of the SEAL to stand near Blade's window. ''Yep. Just killed an eight-point buck this morning. There's lots of deer in these parts.''

Blade allowed his left arm to casually dangle out the window while gripping the Commando with his right hand. ''You have a lot of mouths to feed,'' he remarked.

''We truly do,'' Hefty acknowledged. ''And it ain't easy, let me tell you.''

Blade pointed at the encampment, which began approximately 15 yards to the rear of the men. ''Are you their leader?''

''You could say that,'' Hefty admitted with a smirk.

''How long have you been camped here?''

''Oh, a couple of months.''

''I'm surprised to find your camp near the highway, in the open,'' Blade said. ''Aren't you concerned the Russians might discover it?''

''The Reds don't come this far north much,'' Hefty said. ''We've seen a helicopter or two of theirs, but they left us alone. Didn't want to waste the ammo, I guess.''

Blade stared at the man. ''What would you take in trade for some fresh venison?''

''Do you have any guns in there?'' Hefty asked, tilting his head and trying to peer inside.

''We won't trade guns,'' Blade said.

''What *will* you trade, stranger?''

''We have a spare canteen, several boxes of matches, and a hatchet,'' Blade disclosed. ''Would you be interested in any of those?''

''We could use all of it.''

''I'll trade you the canteen and a box of matches for three venison steaks,'' Blade offered.

Hefty made a show of scratching his stubbly chin. ''Throw in the hatchet.''

"The hatchet and a box of matches," Blade amended.

"No. We'll take the canteen, the matches, and the hatchet," Hefty said.

"We don't need the entire buck," Blade said wryly.

Hefty grinned. "You're a tough customer, that's plain to see." He nodded toward the encampment. "Tell you what. Why don't you and whoever else is in that contraption come out and join us in a brew. We can talk over the trade cordial-like."

"Don't mind if we do," Blade said, and he saw the five men visibly relax. They were undoubtedly convinced they had pulled the wool over his eyes.

"Just park your van over there," Hefty said, indicating a patch of grass between two tents.

"All right," Blade said, then paused. "Say, I've been meaning to ask you a question."

"What's that, stranger?"

"I couldn't help but notice those vehicles in the trees," Blade said innocently. "Where did they come from?"

Hefty frowned. "You're real observant, mister."

"Are they yours?" Blade inquired.

"Yeah," Hefty said, glancing at his four companions.

"Why are they parked in the trees?" Blade pressed him.

"Uhhhh," Hefty began, his forehead creasing. "We don't want the Reds to spot them."

"But you just said the Russians rarely travel this far north of their lines," Blade stated.

"You never know," Hefty responded nervously.

"Would there be another reason those vehicles are in the trees?"

Hefty licked his thick lips. "Like what?"

Blade smiled, drawing the Commando to his chest, the tip of the barrel inches from the window but concealed from the quintet. "Oh, like maybe you hid the vehicles because you don't want anyone to see the bullet holes."

"What bullet holes?" Hefty queried, beginning to elevate the 30-30.

''The bullet holes your buddies and you put there when you killed the people inside those vehicles,'' Blade stated harshly. ''So you could take all of their possessions.''

Hefty glared at the giant. ''You're too damn smart for your own good, stranger!'' he snapped.

And all five men raised their rifles.

Chapter Four

Blade's lightning reflexes were more than equal to the occasion. He simply slid the Commando's barrel over the lower rim of the window and squeezed the trigger. A torrent of slugs slammed into Hefty's chest and smashed him to the fissure-ridden asphalt, geysers of blood spurting from his torso.

On the passenger side, Hickok leaned out of the window and fired each Colt. Two of the men dropped, their craniums shattered.

The remaining pair were back pedaling frantically, shooting as they went, their shots deflected by the SEAL's impenetrable windshield.

Blade and Hickok ducked inside.

"What say we teach these cow-chips a lesson?" the gunman asked.

"Take this," Blade said, extending the Commando to Geronimo with his right arm as he rolled up the window with his left.

"Look at 'em!" Hickok said, following Blade's example.

The scavengers were charging the SEAL en masse, except for the children and a few of the women, who were fleeing into the woods. Dozens of guns were firing simultaneously, and round after round ricocheted off the transport with a loud, pinging sound.

Blade saw the scavengers converging on the highway directly ahead, evidently intending to block the SEAL's path. He glanced at the vehicles in the trees, thinking of the unfortunate victims previously slain by the mob rushing toward him, and his features hardened grimly. He reached to his right and flicked the silver toggle marked with an M.

The scavengers nearest the SEAL were astonished to see metal plates underneath the headlights slide upward, exposing the 50-caliber machine guns in their recessed compartments.

"Look out!" one of the men shouted.

Too late.

Thundering death and destruction, the 50-calibers decimated the foremost ranks in seconds. Men and women toppled to the roadway, screeching and wailing. The scavengers behind the front rows tried to flee, but their limbs could not outrun the heavy slugs. They dropped where they stood, their bodies perforated, spilling their life's blood on the unyielding pavement. Four of the scavengers darted to the right, sprinting toward a shack.

Blade angled the SEAL to the right and applied the brakes again.

The fleeing scavengers were each struck in the back and flung to the ground.

"Got the varmints!" Hickok said.

Blade switched the toggle off and the machine guns ceased chattering. He gazed at the bleeding forms littering the highway, many of whom were moaning or crying. A brunette was convulsing and spitting crimson down her chin. An elderly man was trying to regain his footing, an impossible feat because his left leg was missing below the knee.

"They had it comin'," Hickok remarked.

"Did they?" Geronimo asked.

The gunman looked over his left shoulder. "What's with you?"

"Who appointed us their executioners?"

Hickok knit his brow, perplexed. "You're beginning to sound like Joshua. They were tryin' to kill us, pard, or didn't you notice?"

"They couldn't hurt us in the SEAL," Geronimo said.

"They didn't know that," Hickok stated testily.

"Those people were murderers and thieves," Blade interjected. "Who knows how many people they've killed? Sure, we could have bypassed them without a fight, leaving them free to continue their depredations. And the life of every person they killed from now on would be on our shoulders."

"So there," Hickok said.

"I guess you're right," Geronimo responded.

"What's gotten into you?" Hickok inquired. "You never got upset about blowin' away cow-chips before."

"Some of those scavengers had children," Geronimo said.

"So? Rattlesnakes have young'uns too."

"So I have a son now," Geronimo mentioned. "I see things differently."

Blade twisted in his seat. "Why didn't you tell me?"

Geronimo shrugged. "I didn't want to mention anything until I made my decision."

"What decision?" Hickok asked.

"Whether to resign from the Warriors," Geronimo answered.

Blade and Hickok exchanged flabbergasted expressions.

"You're kiddin'!" the gunman blurted.

"I'm quite serious," Geronimo said. "I've been considering the matter for some time."

"You can't quit!" Hickok exclaimed. "The three of us are best buddies. We're a team. Alpha Triad wouldn't be the same without you."

"The Elders would select a new Warrior to replace me," Geronimo said. "You know the procedure as well as I."

"I know you were born to be a Warrior, just like me," Hickok asserted. "It's in your blood."

"My family must come first."

"You're out of practice," Hickok said. "You haven't been on a run in a spell. Give yourself a few more days. Once you've plugged a few lowlifes, you'll feel a lot better."

"I don't think so," Geronimo replied.

"All right. You sit back and take it easy this trip. I'll do your share of the killin'. Heck, I don't mind. I never sweat the small stuff."

"Small stuff?"

Blade faced front and drove forward, steering the SEAL to the left, skirting the figures cluttering the road. The transport's massive tires pulverized two tents and reduced a crude wooden shack to kindling, and then they were past the scavengers. He slewed onto Highway 24 and resumed their journey.

"I didn't mean to spring this on you," Geronimo said after a minute. "I knew you'd be upset."

"Upset? Who's upset?" Hickok snapped, then lowered his voice. "I think I'll toss Josh in the moat when we get back."

"Joshua had nothing to do with the way I feel," Geronimo said.

"What's your real reason?" Blade inquired. "You've never displayed any reservations about killing in the past. You know as well as we do that killing is part of our duty as Warriors. Sometimes it's a distasteful part, but it must be done. We're a lot like the prewar law-enforcement officers. They had to keep the lid on a society falling apart at the seams, and they had to protect the decent, law-abiding citizens from the predators and vultures. On occasion they had to kill. They might not want to squeeze the trigger, they might try to avoid doing so at all costs, but in the final analysis, those officers, just like the Warriors, had to confront the prospect of killing every day." He paused. "You've been an outstanding Warrior for years. It's not the killing that bothers you. What is it?"

Geronimo sighed and gazed to the right at the forested landscape. "Cynthia and Cochise."

"What about them?" Hickok questioned. "Do they want you to quit?"

"No."

"Then what?" Hickok asked impatiently.

"What happens to them if I'm slain?"

Blade stared into the rearview mirror at Geronimo's reflection, regarding his friend's troubled expression. "The possibility of being killed in the line of duty is an occupational hazard of our profession."

"I know."

"But?" Blade prompted.

"But do I have the right to expose my family to the same hazard?" Geronimo queried. His shoulders slumped. "I never told you this, but Cynthia was a nervous wreck when I returned from our run to Nevada. She hardly slept a wink the whole time we were gone. Cochise was even worse. He started having nightmares, and he would wake up in the middle of the night screaming my name. He's still having nightmares occasionally, and he's scared of his own shadow."

"Have you discussed the situation with them?" Blade inquired.

"Of course. Cynthia admits that she's excessively worried about the likelihood of my being killed. She can't help herself. And as far as Cochise is concerned, what do you say to a three-year-old? How do I explain my extended absences?" Geronimo wanted to know, his tone betraying his profound inner turmoil.

"They'll come around eventually," Hickok said.

"I'm not so sure," Geronimo replied.

"Have you mentioned resigning to Cynthia?" Blade questioned.

"Yes."

"And?"

"And she doesn't want me to resign on account of them."

"The lady has brains," Hickok stated. "You should listen to her."

"I am, with my heart."

"Have you made your final decision yet?" Blade asked.

Geronimo shook his head. "No. I'm leaning toward resigning, though."

"Good. Then I've got time to help you see the light, pard. When we get back, I'll talk to your missus too," Hickok proposed.

"This is personal, Nathan," Geronimo said, using the name bestowed on the gunman by his parents. "I'll handle it."

"Fine. Be that way," Hickok said.

"No offense meant," Geronimo commented.

"None taken," Hickok said, his tone contradicting his words.

They drove on in an uncomfortable silence for several minutes. Finally Hickok turned and stared at Geronimo.

"I think you'll be makin' the biggest mistake of your life if you resign."

"Why?"

"You'll be miserable if you step down," the gunman predicted. "What else would you do?"

"I'm considering becoming a Tiller," Geronimo divulged.

The gunman shook his head. "Never happen. You like excitement and adventure. Sittin' around watching plants grow would bore you to tears."

"I could become a Hunter," Geronimo proposed. "I like hunting and trapping, and providing meat for the Family is a worthy occupation."

"In that case, you might as well stay a Warrior."

"What do you mean?"

"The Hunters go up against mutants and wild critters every time they go out of the Home," Hickok said. "You could be killed just as easily."

"But the Hunters don't venture as far from the Home as we do," Geronimo argued. "The Hunters don't usually take on cannibals or professional assassins or insane power-mongers. I'd be safer as a Hunter."

"If you want to play it safe, become a Weaver."

"I never expected bitterness from you," Geronimo told the

gunman.

"I'm not bitter. I'm just ticked off," Hickok asserted.

"We've got company," Blade announced abruptly.

Hickok straightened and grabbed the AR-15. "Where?"

"Behind us, about three quarters of a mile." Blade informed them.

Hickok looked out the rear of the SEAL, his blue eyes widening slightly as he spied a large, green, single-rotor helicopter. "How long has that contraption been there?"

"I just noticed it," Blade said.

"Russian?"

"It must be," Blade deduced, "but I haven't seen any markings."

"Who else would have a helicopter in this area?" Geronimo queried.

"No one, to my knowledge," Blade responded. He glanced at the side mirror repeatedly as the SEAL covered another mile, expecting the chopper to draw closer rapidly. Instead, the craft kept its distance.

"Why is it hangin' back?" Hickok asked.

"Who knows?" Blade said.

A rusted sign appeared at the side of the highway: WATSEKA 1 MILE.

"Will we go through the town?" Geronimo inquired.

"We'll bypass Watseka," Blade replied. He preferred to avoid cities and towns whenever possible. Prior experience had taught him that the inhabitants of urban centers were invariably hostile, and although most of the dwellers in the Outlands were poorly armed and ill-equipped to cause any serious damage to the SEAL, he wanted to avoid unnecessary confrontations and delays.

"Look!" Hickok suddenly declared, pointing at the sky to the east.

Blade glanced up and tensed.

A second helicopter was less than a half mile distant and heading directly toward the transport.

Chapter Five

"They've got us hemmed in," Hickok said.

Blade braked the SEAL, peering intently at the oncoming chopper, striving to identify the model. His knowledge of aircraft was relatively limited, and he resolved to brush up on the various types of helicopters by studying the appropriate books in the Family library at the first opportunity.

"The copter behind us is closing in," Geronimo disclosed.

A quick check of the side mirror confirmed the helicopters were working in tandem.

"The old squeeze play," Hickok remarked.

Blade reached toward the silver toggles, then hesitated.

"What are you waitin' for?" Hickok demanded. "Sic the Stinger on one of them."

"We don't know if they're hostile," Blade said.

"Better safe than sorry," the gunman noted.

The chopper to the east was swooping at the SEAL, its rotor blades shimmering in the sunlight.

"We're sittin' ducks if we stay put," Hickok cautioned.

Blade wrenched the steering wheel to the left and pressed on the accelerator, intending to drive the transport into the shelter of the woods. Even as he did, there was a puff of smoke and a brief burst of flame shot from under the helicopter in front of the SEAL.

"They've fired a rocket!" Geronimo exclaimed.

Forty feet from the SEAL a section of Highway 24 exploded, showering dirt, dust, and chunks of asphalt in all directions. The transport swayed but stayed on course, bouncing as it left the roadway and sped toward the nearest trees.

Blade pressed the toggle labeled with an S. He knew a panel in the roof above him was opening, and he felt the SEAL lurch as the heat-seeking, surface-to-air missile was launched.

"I can see it!" Hickok cried, his face pressed to the windshield.

Blade glanced to the right, and he was able to glimpse the glistening Stinger as the missile arced toward the helicopter to the east. The next moment he was forced to devote his full attention to driving. The SEAL entered the forest, narrowly missing a towering oak tree. He skillfully manipulated the steering wheel, threading a path among the tree trunks, the transport flattening the underbrush in its path.

"One down!" Hickok exclaimed.

A resounding blast flared in the eastern sky, and a cloud of smoke and fire engulfed the second helicopter.

Blade slammed on the brakes and craned his neck. He could see the crumpled chopper, a gaping, ragged hole in its side, plummeting earthward, its rotor blades twisted, spewing black smoke. The helicopter crashed into the trees less than 300 yards off, and a column of fire and smoke erupted toward the heavens.

"The other one has stopped," Geronimo said.

Blade turned and gazed to the west. The first chopper was hovering 500 yards from the transport. Would the pilot decide to attack? The SEAL possessed the capability to fire just one Stinger at a time. A spare was stored in the rear section, but to mount the missile entailed climbing onto the roof using a ladder affixed to the back of the vehicle. Anyone trying to do so would be easy prey for the chopper.

"Here it comes," Geronimo declared.

"Out of the SEAL," Blade ordered, and threw open his door. He dropped to the ground with the Commando in his right hand, then slammed the door shut.

Hickok and Geronimo jumped down on the passenger side, then came around the front.

"What's your plan, pard?" the gunman asked.

Blade was watching the helicopter, which was flying slowly in their general direction. The pilot was keeping the aircraft 50 feet above the treetops, swerving from side to side, evidently searching for the SEAL. The canopy of branches and leaves screened the forest floor from aerial observation.

"Do we take it down?" Hickok queried hopefully.

"We do," Blade confirmed. "Take cover. Wait until I give the word."

The Warriors fanned out, taking up positions behind nearby trees.

Blade crouched in the shelter of a Norway maple and pressed the Commando to his right shoulder. He could hear the whump-whump-whump of the craft's rotors as the helicopter drew to within 40 yards of his position. A cool breeze stirred his dark hair. He stared through the branches and spotted a bright red marking on the right side of the chopper.

A solitary star above a crossed hammer and sickle.

Definitely Russian.

Blade sighted the Commando on the forward fuselage, his finger on the trigger. He wanted the helicopter as close as possible before he fired. As he waited, scarcely breathing in anticipation, a disturbing thought sprang into his mind: The Soviet pilots must have contacted their superiors. Odds were, one or both of the pilots had radioed the nearest Red air base to report the presence of the green van. The Russians undoubtedly knew about the SEAL. Would a sharp officer recognize the Family's unique vehicle from the description given by the pilots? If so, the Reds might put their border units on alert and advise their patrols to be on the lookout for the SEAL.

The helicopter was now 30 yards from the Warriors, its elongated body fully visible. A sliding door was open, exposing a wide bay on the side. Framed in the doorway was a machine gunner.

Blade waited. He saw the machine gunner surveying the woods below.

That's it.

Just a little bit closer.

The rotors were creating a loud clamor, and the wind generated by the rotating blades was bending the tops of the trees.

A little closer.

Blade saw the machine gunner's head snap to the right.

The Russian had spotted the SEAL!

"Now!" Blade bellowed, and fired, the Commando thundering and bucking.

Geronimo and Hickok cut loose.

The cockpit windows dissolved into shattered shards, and a second later the helicopter banked to the south. Undaunted, the machine gunner sent a burst into the trees in the vicinity of the SEAL.

Blade aimed at the soldier and squeezed the trigger.

A dozen rounds struck the Russian in the chest, and he was hurled backwards into the helicopter.

Hickok suddenly stepped into the open, into a small clearing, the AR-15 elevated, going for the chopper's tail rotor. He fired four times.

The Soviet helicopter was speeding southward, and the craft abruptly started weaving, its tail out of control.

"Piece of cake!" Hickok declared, elated.

Blade walked to the gunman's side. "Nice shooting."

"What else?"

A thin plume of white smoke paced the helicopter's passage through the blue sky. The tail section seemed to stabilize slightly, and the chopper pursued a steadier course.

"Crash, blast you!" Hickok said.

The Russian craft continued on a beeline toward the Soviet territory. In less than a minute the helicopter was lost to the view of the Warriors.

"Darn," Hickok muttered.

Geronimo joined them. "They'll be expecting us in Cincinnati," he mentioned.

"Maybe not," Blade disagreed. "They know we're here, but they don't know where we're headed. For all they know, our destination is somewhere in the Outlands."

"Who cares if they know or not?" Hickok asked. "We have a job to do, and we always get the job done."

"We keep going then?" Geronimo inquired.

Blade nodded.

Geronimo's mouth curved downward, but he held his tongue.

"Let's go," Blade said.

They returned to the SEAL.

"Now where were we?" Hickok queried as they climbed inside.

"We were discussing my resignation from the Warriors," Geronimo reminded him.

"Let's drop the subject for now," Blade suggested. He placed his Commando on the console, then started the SEAL.

"Is there something else you'd rather discuss?" Geronimo questioned.

"We need to talk about Cincinnati," Blade said, pulling out.

"What about it?" came from Hickok.

"The Russians have the city under their control. You and I have been in Soviet-occupied territory before, so we have some idea of what to expect. There will be troops everywhere. We can't simply barge into the city and expect to accomplish our mission. We've got to use our heads," Blade stated.

"That leaves Hickok out," Geronimo quipped.

"We can hide the SEAL a few miles from the city and proceed on foot," Blade said. "But if we try to enter during daylight, we're bound to arouse suspicion, dressed as we are."

"Speak for yourself," Hickok commented. "My duds are the height of fashion."

Blade concentrated on avoiding a tree as he headed for Highway 24. "We could try to enter the city at night, when we'd be less likely to stand out, but we'd still have a problem."

"Our weapons," Geronimo said.

"You've got it. Only Russian soldiers are permitted to carry weapons," Blade noted. "They would pounce on any armed civilians." He paused. "I'm not about to go in there unarmed."

"Then what do we do?" Hickok asked.

"We find a Soviet squad and persuade them to lend us their uniforms," Blade stated.

Hickok chuckled.

"With Russian uniforms on, we should be able to walk around unchallenged," Blade said.

"You hope," Geronimo remarked.

"Don't worry, pard," Hickok declared. "We'll be in and out before the Commies know what hit them."

Chapter Six

The full moon cast the nighttime terrain in a pale glow.

"Looks like a farmhouse," Hickok said.

Blade nodded, surveying the farm below, noting the three-story house to the north, the barn to the east, and the fenced pasture containing a herd of cattle to the south. He looked to his right at the gunman, then to his left at Geronimo. The three of them were on a rise 60 yards to the west of the farm, lying prone with their heads above the rim, a forest to their rear. "Let's pay the owners a visit," he directed, bracing his palms on the grass.

"Wait," Geronimo stated, pointing at the porch bordering the south side of the farmhouse. "There are dogs."

"I don't see any," Hickok said.

"Wait a moment," Geronimo advised, placing the SAR on the ground.

Blade was straining to perceive the dogs, thankful for Geronimo's excellent vision. All of Geronimo's senses were above average, and Blade wondered if the fact was attributable to his friend's Blackfoot inheritance. He detected movement near the house, and two dogs appeared in a circle of light radiated by a lamp attached to a porch post.

"They'll raise a ruckus if we try to get closer," Hickok whispered. "Do we take them out?"

Blade pursed his lips, deliberating. Three hours remained until dawn, and he estimated they were still over 20 miles north of Cincinnati. The SEAL was concealed in dense woods seven miles to the northwest, not far from State Highway 725. "Yes, but we don't kill them."

"Have you gone loco?" Hickok responded. "How the blazes will we do that?" His right elbow bumped the AR-15 lying at his side.

"I have an idea," Blade said, and sat up. He began undoing the laces on his left combat boot.

"I've got it!" Hickok stated with a smirk. "We'll let 'em get a whiff of your feet and they'll keel right over."

Blade removed the lace from his left boot.

"Are you aimin' to take those clodhoppers off?" Hickok asked.

"Yep."

"Darn. And I forgot to bring my gas mask."

"Keep it up," Blade said, working on his right boot.

Geronimo looked at the gunman. "Does this qualify as cruelty to animals?"

"Forget the critters. What about us?"

Blade pulled the right lace free. "Here," he said, and gave it to the gunfighter.

Hickok studied the black lace for a second. "Am I supposed to lasso one of the dogs with this?"

"Remind me to bring Yama on the next run. He doesn't talk as much," Blade retorted, and handed the left lace to Geronimo. He stripped his boots off and gazed at the farmhouse.

The dogs were sitting at the base of the steps leading onto the porch.

"I don't want to kill the farmer's dogs if it can be helped,"

Blade explained. "The farmer will be less likely to cooperate if we slay them."

"We're going to tie their tails together so they can't go anywhere," Hickok guessed sarcastically.

Blade took off his combat boots and rose to his knees. "When I grab the dogs, I want you to tie their mouths shut."

Hickok glanced at Geronimo. "Next he'll have us wrestling worms."

Blade sighed and motioned with his arms at the ground. "Stay down, and don't make a peep."

They complied.

"Here goes nothing," Blade said, and whistled as loud as he could.

Reacting instantly, the dogs stood on all fours and stared in the direction of the rise.

Blade repeated the whistle. How keen was their eyesight? If they couldn't see him, would they come to investigate? If they started barking now and woke up the householders, the jig would be up and the Warriors would have to move on. He could see wires leading into the house from a pole next to the curved front drive, and he concluded the people must possess a telephone. Neutralizing the dogs was imperative if he wanted to subdue the occupants quietly before they could use the phone. He didn't want to cut the wires.

The largest dog advanced several yards toward the rise, its head upraised, apparently sniffing the air.

Nice try, dog, Blade thought, but the wind was blowing his scent away from the farm. He whistled a third time, lower than before.

Both dogs jogged to the west.

Blade smiled and reached into his left front pocket for a stick of venison jerky. The Commando was on the grass behind him so the canines wouldn't be spooked by the oily, metallic scent of his firearm. He squinted, focusing on the dark shapes bounding across the field separating the farmhouse from the rise.

The dogs came on rapidly.

Blade whistled the tune to "Old MacDonald" softly while breaking the stick of jerky into small pieces which he clasped in his left hand. He adopted an air of supreme nonchalance, not even bothering to watch the dogs. Any hint of hostility on his part, and the dogs would be on him tooth and nail. He wanted to lull them into a false sense of security, to convince them he was harmless.

The padding of their feet reached his ears.

He intentionally stayed on his knees. The dogs might be too wary to draw near if he straightened to his full seven-foot height. He whistled and waited, gazing at his thighs.

A low growl heralded their arrival.

Blade calmly looked up, discovering the pair 20 feet off, eyeing him balefully. Both were mixed breeds, mongrels. The large dog was brown, the smaller black and white. He placed a piece of jerky in his mouth and chewed noisily, smacking his lips and saying "Ummmmm," repeatedly.

The dogs inched closer.

He gazed at them and smiled.

Both dogs snarled.

Blade grinned and pretended to put another morsel of jerky into his mouth. He acted like it was the best meat he'd ever tasted.

The brown dog took several steps closer.

Here goes nothing, Blade told himself, and tossed a piece of venison at the large dog. The jerky landed a foot short.

Predictably, the farm dogs retreated several yards, bristling and growling.

Blade ignored them, continuing to champ and smack his lips. He held his arms at his sides to avoid frightening them. The seconds stretched into a minute. Two.

The large dog moved cautiously forward, smelling the grass, until it found the scrap of venison. One hungry gulp and the jerky was gone.

Blade smiled and whistled, casually flinging another piece midway between the big dog and himself.

Torn between its appetite and its instinctive wariness, the

dog looked from the Warrior to the jerky and back again. Appetite won.

"Good boy," Blade said softly. "Good boy."

The dog's tail wagged.

Blade threw a third chunk of venison out.

Apparently not content to allow its companion to get all the food, the small dog darted forward and wolfed down the chunk.

"You guys are starved," Blade addressed them in a composed tone. "Here." He pitched two pieces a yard from his legs.

The dogs were on the meat in a flash. They swallowed without chewing, then stared at him, wanting more.

"Good dogs," Blade said. "Treat yourselves." He dropped two morsels near his knees and tensed.

They came nearer tentatively and ate the meat.

Blade was down to his last two pieces, and he was ready to make his move. He could feel their fetid breath on his skin. Neither of the canines were displaying any aggression, but they could revert at a moment's notice. He would have a split second to succeed; if he missed, there would not be a second chance.

The small dog whined expectantly, craving additional venison.

"Here you go," Blade whispered, and let the last morsels fall next to his kneecaps. He placed his hands on his legs just above his knees. "Enjoy yourselves."

They hesitated, then stepped closer and snapped at the venison, lowering their muzzles to the grass and exposing the backs of their necks.

Now!

Blade's hands flashed out, his steely fingers clamping on each dog behind the ears, his sinews bulging as he gripped the folds of their skin and heaved erect.

Both dogs automatically tried to pull from his grasp, and as their front legs were hauled from the ground they endeavored to bite the arms holding them, snarling viciously, their fangs exposed.

Blade whipped each hand outward, spinning the dogs away from his body. "Tie them before they bark!" he ordered.

Hickok and Geronimo materialized in front of him. The small dog had gone unexpectedly limp, trembling with fear, and Geronimo easily looped a lace tightly around its mouth. Hickok, however, was having problems. The large dog growled, thrashed, and bit at the gunman's hands.

"Hold still, you mangy mutt!"

"Hurry," Blade stated.

Hickok tried once more, and narrowly missed losing a finger to the dog's wicked teeth. "So you want to play rough?" he said, and leaned over, inspecting the area between the dog's rear legs.

"What in the world are you doing?" Blade inquired.

"I just wanted to see if this critter is a guy or a girl," Hickok explained. "It's a male."

"What difference does its sex make?" Geronimo asked.

"Plenty," the gunman replied, and slugged the dog in the jewels.

The dog uttered a peculiar gurgling noise, whined, and sagged in Blade's hands.

Hickok grinned and secured the lace about the dog's mouth. "There."

Blade felt the dog quivering in agony. "I don't recall being taught that ploy in our Warrior classes."

"I picked it up from Lynx," Hickok divulged.

Blade smiled. Lynx was one of three mutant Warriors, all of whom were outcasts the Family had adopted. "It figures," he said.

"Lynx has a motto I kind of like," Hickok elaborated. "He says it comes in handy in any kind of fight."

"What's the motto?" Geronimo queried.

"When in doubt, go for the gonads."

"I thought you always go for the head."

Hickok shrugged. "A fellow should always have a backup strategy," he mentioned.

Blade headed toward the farmhouse. "One of you bring my boots and the Commando."

"You take the boots," Geronimo said to the gunman.

"I'll carry the long guns," Hickok offered, and moved to the Colt AR-15.

"I'll carry them," Geronimo proposed.

Fifteen feet off, Blade halted and glanced over his right shoulder, a docile dog in each huge hand. "I don't care which one brings the guns and which one brings the boots. Just do it."

"Goody," Hickok said, and scooped up the weapons. He smirked at Geronimo and hurried after the giant.

Geronimo retrieved the combat boots and caught up with them. "I owe you one, Nathan."

"What'd I do?" Hickok asked with all the innocence of a newborn baby.

"I owe you," Geronimo reiterated.

The Warriors crossed the field to the edge of a wide lawn dotted with trees and shrubs. They stopped behind a short, squat pine tree. Geronimo promptly deposited the boots on the grass.

"Hickok, I want you to check out the barn," Blade commanded. "Look for some rope."

Hickok nodded, handed the SAR and Commando to Geronimo, and ran toward the barn.

"Do you want me to cut the wires?" Geronimo queried.

"Not yet," Blade said. "Someone might try to call these people in the morning, and we wouldn't want the caller to become suspicious and alert the authorities."

They waited for the gunman, listening to the breeze rustling the limbs. In the quiet hours preceding the dawn, the farm was tranquil, the picture of serenity.

Geronimo stared at Blade.

"Something wrong?" the giant whispered.

"Why didn't you kill the dogs?"

"I told you. I don't want to antagonize the people living here."

"Are you sure that's the only reason?"

"Why else?"

"Oh, like maybe you didn't want to upset me."

Blade looked at the farmhouse. "Ridiculous."

"The easy way would have been to slit their throats with your Bowies," Geronimo noted.

"They weren't a threat."

"They could have barked and given us away. Are you trying to avoid spilling blood for my benefit?"

"Would I do that?"

"Yes," Geronimo answered. "You're one of my best friends. You might try to go easy on the killing this trip, hoping I'll forget all about the idea of resigning."

"I'm not that devious."

"Yes, you are. Hickok isn't. He'll stay on my case until I agree to remain a Warrior. But you'll use your head. You'll try psychology on me."

"You overestimate my ability."

"And you weren't selected to be the head of the Warriors because of your stinky feet."

"What do you guys have against my feet?"

"Don't change the subject. I want to know your honest feelings. Would my quitting be a mistake, like Nathan claims?"

Blade looked at Geronimo. "The decision must be yours."

"But how do you feel?"

"Do you really want to step down?"

Geronimo averted his eyes.

"Do you?" Blade pressed him.

"No."

"I didn't think so. But you'll resign for the sake of your family."

"My family's happiness must come first."

"I agree."

"What would you do?"

"Do you want an honest answer?"

"I'd expect nothing less," Geronimo said.

Blade frowned, allowing his arms to droop. The small dog

was whining, but the large one hadn't so much as whimpered since Hickok's lesson in behavior modification. "I haven't told anyone else this. I've been thinking about resigning too."

Geronimo was shocked. "What?" he blurted.

"As you know, I'm also the head of the Freedom Force based in Los Angeles. The strain on my family has been severe, what with my constant commuting between the Home and California. Even when I'm at the Home, I'm always being sent on missions to deal with the latest threat to our Family's safety. I'd rather spend the time with Jenny and Gabe."

"And you're seriously thinking about quitting?"

"I am."

"What will Plato think?"

"I love Plato like a father, but he isn't married to Jenny. The decision is mine," Blade stated.

Geronimo abruptly glanced to the east. "Hickok is coming, but he's not alone."

"He's not?" Blade said, starting to turn, and as he did a chorus of bestial howls rent the night.

Chapter Seven

More damn dogs!

Blade could see the gunman racing in their direction, his legs flying, while on Hickok's trail came a baying pack of mongrel hounds, five all told. The two in his hands were just members of a pack! Now the people in the farmhouse were bound to wake up! Infuriated, he rammed the heads of the large and small dogs together, stunning them, and cast them to the grass. He whipped out his Bowies and faced the onrushing pack. "No guns," he instructed Geronimo, who promptly lowered the SAR and the Commando and drew his tomahawk.

A wide grin was plastered on Hickok's countenance as he drew near. "Company's comin'," he announced, then slowed and gripped the Colt AR-15 by the barrel.

The five farm dogs never slowed.

Hickok took down the first dog, a huge beast, with a terrific swing of the AR-15, the stock crashing into the dog's cranium and checking its leap at his legs.

A pair of brutish canines swerved at Blade.

The giant Warrior was ready, his legs braced, a Bowie in each hand. He did the unexpected, moving to meet them, his arms sweeping up and in as they launched themselves simultaneously. The Bowies arced in low, taking each dog in the chest, imbedding to their hilts. The dog on his left slumped over, but the one on the right voiced a plaintive howl before collapsing, its blood spilling over his hand. He glanced at Geronimo.

A dog was dead on the grass at Geronimo's feet, its head split open, and as Blade watched, a second dog was met in midair by the light axe used so extensively by Geronimo's Blackfeet ancestors. The dog's cranium was rent from forehead to nose, and the animal fell soundlessly.

"I bumped into these critters near the barn," Hickok explained.

Blade swung his arms outwards, dislodging the dogs from his Bowies, and turned toward the house. Sure enough, a light had come on in a second-floor window. "I want these people alive if possible," he advised, and nodded at the house.

Hickok circled to the right, Geronimo the left with the SAR.

Blade dashed up to the front porch, his socks making no noise on the grass, and bounded onto the steps. He was a stride from the wooden door when lights went on downstairs. With a leap he was to the right of the door, his back to the wall, the crimson-soaked Bowies ready.

The doorknob twisted, and a second later an elderly woman in an ankle-length nightgown emerged onto the porch. "Daffodil?" she called. "Buttercup?"

Blade stepped into the doorway, blocking her retreat. "I'm afraid your dogs were too loud for their own good," he said softly.

She spun, gazing in horror at his face, awed by his stature. Her right hand covered her mouth.

"Don't make a peep," Blade warned.

She didn't.

She swooned instead.

Blade turned, finding a narrow hall and a series of doors.

And two children ten feet away, in their cotton pajamas, gawking.

"It's a monster!" cried a little girl of about seven.

"It's a mutant!" stated her brother, who appeared to be two or three years older.

"I'm a friend," Blade said.

They gaped at the dripping Bowies, screeched, and bolted, fleeing toward stairs at the far end of the hall.

"Mommy!" wailed the girl.

"It's a mutant!" the boy reiterated in stark terror.

Blade raced after them, overtaking the children at the base of the stairs. "Stop!" he commanded.

With a thin leg on the bottom step, each child froze, the girl trembling, the boy gasping for air.

"I won't hurt you," Blade assured them.

"Damn straight you won't, mister!" snapped a harsh feminine voice above him.

Blade looked up.

A woman in her thirties was standing on the seventh step, her attractive features set in grim lines, her brown hair in a bun, and a cocked double-barreled shotgun in her hands, pointed at the Warrior's chest. She was wearing a blue robe. "One twitch and you're dead!"

"I mean you no harm," Blade told her.

"Sure you don't, you son of a bitch!" She glanced at his Bowies, at the blood, and glared into his eyes. "You killed my Momma!"

Blade threw himself to the right.

The blast of the twin barrels was deafening in the confined hallway. The buckshot narrowly missed the children and blew a jagged hole the size of a watermelon in the wall on the opposite side. Both children screamed.

Stepping into the open, Blade raised his right arm as if to throw the Bowie. "Freeze!" he barked.

The woman had snapped the shotgun open and was fumbling in the left pocket in her robe for more shells. She stood still, her brown eyes wide with tears in the corners.

"I didn't kill your mother," Blade said. "She fainted on the front porch. She should be fine."

"You're lying!" the woman replied bitterly.

The children were pale, holding hands, like frightened fawns confronted by a snarling cougar.

"Why would I lie?" Blade retorted. "If I wanted to kill you, you'd already be dead. I mean you no harm."

She straightened slowly, the shotgun sagging, clearly bewildered. "You're not going to kill us?"

"All we want is information," Blade said.

"We?"

A door six feet behind Blade opened, and Hickok walked into the hallway, the AR-15 leveled. He took one look and grinned. "Howdy, folks. Sorry my pard here didn't knock, but his manners need workin' on." He strolled over to Blade. "I came in through a window," he said, and glanced at the woman. "You folks really should lock your place up tight at night. You never know what kind of varmints are runnin' loose."

"There's two of you!" she blurted.

"Three," stated a voice to her rear.

The woman spun and nearly lost her balance.

Geronimo stood five steps above her, the SAR trained on the small of her back. He smiled pleasantly. "You should consider trimming the limbs on the tree behind your house. One of them comes within inches of your bedroom window."

"Who the hell are you?" she demanded. "What the hell are you sons of bitches doing in our house?"

"If you don't mind my sayin' so, ma'am," Hickok said indignantly, "that's no way for a lady to be talkin' in front of the young'uns."

The woman's face became beet red. "Why you . . ." she blurted. "You . . .you . . ."

"The handle is Hickok, at your service," the gunman stated, and bowed.

"What are you *doing* here?"

"First things first," Blade declared, and looked at Hickok.

"I want you to go get my Commando, and check on the mother. See if you can bring her around."

"On my way," Hickok said, taking a stride and looking down at Blade's feet. "I'll also fetch your boots and laces. We don't want to fluster these folks more than we already have." He moved past the giant to the front door.

The little girl stared at Blade's feet. "Golly. Those are the biggest feet in the whole world."

"He must be part mutant," her older brother speculated.

Geronimo started laughing.

The mother glanced from the Indian to the giant. "Lunatics! We've been invaded by lunatics!"

"Where can we talk?" Blade asked. "I want all of us in the same room."

"There's the living room," she suggested.

"Okay. We'll go to the living room. But first, hand the shotgun to my friend," Blade directed.

She turned and extended the gun.

"Thank you," Geronimo said, taking the weapon in his left hand.

"What's your name?" Blade asked her.

"Eberle. Holly Eberle," she said, stepping down the stairs and placing a hand on each of her children. "My daughter's name is Claudia, and my son is Danny. Please don't hurt us."

"I've already told you that we're not going to hurt you," Blade reminded her.

Holly glanced at the Bowies. "Where'd the blood come from?"

Blade frowned and hefted the knives. "I'm afraid we had to kill some of your dogs."

"Our dogs!" Danny exclaimed, and tried to move toward the front door.

"Stay put!" Holly snapped, gripping his right shoulder. "We don't want to make these men angry, honey."

Danny looked up at her. "But mom, they killed our dogs! They killed Buttercup!"

"We didn't kill all of your dogs," Blade said, guilt racking him as he beheld the boy's horrified features. "There was a large brown dog and a small black and white one—"

"That's Daffodil!" cried Danny. "And the brown one must be Buttercup!"

"Daffodil and Buttercup are okay," Blade declared. "They don't have a scratch on them."

Danny's accusing brown eyes bored into the Warrior's. "You swear to God you didn't hurt them?"

"They're fine," Blade reiterated. "You can see for yourself shortly." He looked at Holly. "Lead the way to the living room."

Holly and the children edged past the giant cautiously, Claudia gazing at Blade as if he was the worst monster on the face of the planet. "You meanie!" she declared.

Geronimo came down the stairs. "At least Tillers and Hunters don't have people hating their guts."

"Check the house," Blade ordered testily. "Every room, from top to bottom."

"What do I do about this?" Geronimo asked, wagging the shotgun.

Blade wiped the Bowies on his pants, slid the knives into their sheaths, and took the shotgun.

"I'll start upstairs," Geronimo said, and went back up.

"There's no one else here," Holly told Blade.

"We've got to check," the giant said. "We won't disturb any of your property. We're not thieves."

"What, *exactly*, are you?"

"We'll ask the questions," Blade said. "Now where's the living room?"

Holly and the children led the way down the hall to a door on the right, and Holly pushed the door inward and flicked on a light. She escorted her children to a faded blue sofa and seated herself between them, hugging them close.

Blade walked to a rocking chair on the left and leaned the shotgun against an arm. "I'll make this short and sweet. Answer me honestly and we'll be out of your hair in no time."

"What do you want to know?" Holly asked.

"Are we behind the Russian lines?"

Holly cocked her head to one side and peered at him quizzically. "You don't know?"

"I believe we are, but the Russians haven't strung barbed wire along their frontier or posted signs," Blade mentioned. "We didn't see any patrols, which doesn't mean a thing because they tend to concentrate most of their troops in the cities. So are we in Soviet-controlled territory or not?"

"Unfortunately, you are," Holly said bitterly.

"Where is the nearest Soviet garrison?"

"Cincinnati."

"That far?"

"They've turned Cincinnati into a military-industrial complex," Holly disclosed. "The city is an armed camp. They send out regular patrols in a fifty-mile radius."

Blade scrutinized the modest furnishings in the living room, the peeling green paint on the walls, the cracks in the plaster coating the ceiling. "The Russians let you keep your own home? I'm surprised they haven't turned your farm into a collective."

"My grandfather told me the Russians tried to organize a collective system after the war," Holly disclosed. "But their scheme didn't work. The farmers wouldn't cooperate, even though many of them were tortured and killed. The city folks didn't know beans about growing crops and couldn't do diddly without help from the farmers. And there weren't enough Russians to enforce the edicts establishing the collectives."

"So the Soviets let the farmers keep their land?"

"In most cases. They did succeed in setting up a few collectives here and there, but for the most part they simply take ninety percent of all the crops the farmers harvest," Holly said.

"They visit you periodically?"

"At least once a week a patrol shows up to check on us," Holly replied. "They keep tabs on the crops, and they send trucks at harvest time to take their fair share." She spoke the last two words with unconcealed rancor.

"You don't sound too happy about the state of affairs," Blade commented.

"Would you be?" Holly responded resentfully. "But there's nothing I can do about it, not after they . . ." she said, and stopped, her eyelids lowering, her lips compressing.

"They what?" Blade prompted.

"They killed my husband," Holly revealed softly.

"I'm sorry."

Holly looked up at him, trying to gauge if he was sincere, and decided he was. "Thanks."

"Care to tell me about it?"

"There are a lot of poor folks around," Holly said. "The people in the cities and the towns receive just enough food to keep them alive. Even the farmers barely get by. My husband, Tim, was part of an underground movement."

"Go on."

Holly studied his rugged features. "I've told you too much already."

"What about this underground movement?"

"How do I know I can trust you?" Holly queried suspiciously. "You might be with the KGB."

"Do you really think I am?"

Before the woman could respond, Hickok sauntered into the living room carrying Blade's combat boot and laces in his left hand. He scrunched up his nose. "Here, pard. Take these before my nose kicks the bucket." The Commando was slung over his left shoulder.

Blade took the boots and sat down in the rocker to put them on.

Holly stared at the gunman. "There's no way *he* could be with the KGB."

"What the dickens is the KGB?" Hickok asked.

"The Committee for State Security," Holly said. "the Soviet secret police."

Hickok chuckled. "I'm not a Commie, ma'am."

"That much is obvious," Holly said. "But where are you from? Why are you here?"

"Shouldn't you be more concerned about your ma?" Hickok rejoined.

Holly appeared shocked. "Damn! How is she?"

"She's snoozin' away on the front porch," Hickok said.

"Bring her inside," Blade instructed.

Hickok deposited the Commando on the floor next to the rocking chair, slung the AR-15 over his right shoulder, and strolled out.

"Tell me more about the underground," Blade stated, sliding his right foot into a combat boot.

"Some of the farmers banded together to try and do something about the food situation," Holly said. "They hide a small portion of the harvest, then smuggle the food into Cincinnati. Not much, mind you, but every little bit helps."

"They put their lives on the line for a handful of grain," Blade remarked.

"That's about it."

"What happened to your husband?"

Holly sighed. "Tim built an underground bin for grain and corn in the southwest corner of one of our fields to the east. There were trees all around, and no one could see the corner from the road. He never expected the Russians to find the bin."

"They did?"

"I don't know how, but they did," Holly said. "It was like they knew where to look." She paused, hugging her children, her countenance a mask of sorrow. "They took him to Cincinnati, tried him, and put him in front of a firing squad."

"But they let you stay on the farm?"

"The Soviet commander of the Cincinnati garrison, General Kasantsev, told me that we could stay as long as our production quota is met. If we're one bushel short, though, we'll be booted off and sent to a relocation camp. I think he allowed us to stay because we know the land so well, and because we were in the middle of the growing season when Tim was executed."

Their conversation was interrupted as Hickok ambled in with the elderly woman cradled gently in his arms.

She was awake, regarding the gunman angrily, her thin

hands on his chest. "Put me down, young man! I'm perfectly capable of walking by myself."

"Mom!" Holly exclaimed, rising and hastening to her mother. "Are you all right?"

"Of course," her mother replied. "Tell this pervert to put me down. I don't like having strangers paw me."

"I'm not a pervert," Hickok said.

"That's a matter of opinion," the mother retorted.

Hickok halted and lowered the woman to the floor. "And I don't go in for pawin' women. My missus would break my fingers if I tried."

"You're married?"

"Yep."

"Your wife has my sympathy."

Holly grabbed her mother's left wrist. "Mom! Don't talk like that."

"I'm not scared of these scavengers," the mother stated.

His combat boots snug on his feet, Blade rose and placed his hands on his hips. "We're not scavengers."

The mother swiveled toward him, her right hand covering her mouth. "Good Lord! I didn't imagine it. You *are* real!"

"What's your name?" Blade inquired.

"Ethel," she answered, gawking, astonished at his size.

"Have a seat," Blade said, indicating the sofa with a jerk of his right thumb.

At that moment Geronimo materialized in the doorway. "You'd better come outside," he informed Blade. "We might have an uninvited visitor."

Chapter Eight

"Watch them," Blade directed Hickok, then snatched the Commando and dashed after Geronimo to the front porch.

"See?" Geronimo said.

Less than a mile to the southeast a pair of headlights were visible, approaching in the general direction of the farmhouse.

"Get Holly," Blade directed.

"You've got it," Geronimo responded, and went indoors.

Blade stared at the circles of light, pondering the implications. The hour was still early, too early for anyone to be abroad, for someone to be paying the Eberles a visit. How far would the noise of the shotgun blast have carried? If a Russian patrol heard the sound, they'd undoubtedly investigate. He intended to jump a Soviet squad and confiscate their uniforms, but he wanted to pick the time and the place.

Geronimo returned with Holly.

"What is it?" she queried.

Blade pointed at the distant headlights. "Is there a road to the south of your farm?"

"A dirt lane leads from our farm to a paved road," Holly

said. "I'd say that vehicle is on the road."

"Are there any other farms nearby? Any turnoffs?"

"Gus Seuell has a farm a quarter of a mile to the east," Holly mentioned. "To get here, he has to swing around to the south. That could be him."

"Why would he be coming here at this time of the morning?" Blade questioned.

"I don't know," Holly said.

"Is this Seuell a close friend of yours?"

"To tell you the truth, I never much liked Gus. Tim and him were good buddies, but he always made me feel uncomfortable," Holly disclosed.

"Why?"

Holly shrugged. "I can't really say. Gus was always nice to me, always considerate. Since Tim was executed, Gus has been over here every day asking if there's anything he can do to help out. I suppose I should like him more, but my intuition bothers me whenever he's around."

"Hmmmmm," was all Blade said.

"Orders?" Geronimo asked.

"Go inside and turn out all the lights," Blade stated. "Have Hickok stay in the living room with the Eberles, except for Holly. She'll be with me. Find a second-floor window and be ready if I give the signal."

"What about the dead dogs?"

"I'll hide them" Blade proposed. "Get going."

Geronimo departed.

"What about me?" Holly queried.

"You can remain on the porch or come with me," Blade said, striding down the steps.

"I'll go with you," Holly said, following. "I must be crazy. You killed most of our dogs, broke into our house, and yet I feel safe around you."

Blade looked at her. "I'm truly sorry about the dogs. I tried to avoid harming them. They didn't leave us any choice."

"Farm dogs are very territorial," Holly commented.

The large brown dog and the small black and white canine

abruptly raced around a yellow poplar tree on the left, growling as they neared the Warrior.

"Daffodil! Buttercup! No!" Holly declared. "Stop!"

They checked their rush, growling and glaring at Blade.

"Go to the barn!" Holly directed. "The barn! Go! Now!"

Buttercup and Daffodil, unwilling but obedient, padded off.

"The barn!" Holly called after them. "Go to the barn!"

"Thanks," Blade said. "I didn't want to kill them too." He walked to the corpses of the five dead dogs.

"Sweet Jesus!" Holly blurted out when she spied the bodies.

Blade slung the Commando over his left arm and grabbed one of the dogs by the scruff of the neck. He lugged the canine to a nearby lilac bush and placed it at the base of the ten-foot high shrub. He arranged the lower branches and leaves to partially screen the dead dog, then stepped back to inspect his handiwork. Unless someone was within a yard or two of the lilac bush, he doubted the corpse could be seen. Working quickly, he brought the other bodies over and hid them in the shadows.

"I'd better bury them before Danny and Claudia see them," Holly remarked.

"We'll bury them before we leave," Blade said, and turned to the southwest. The headlights were a half mile distant, intermittently discernible, their glimmering radiance eclipsed by periodic stands of trees. He glanced at the barn and noticed a driveway on the south side. The gravel drive widened and extended to within 15 yards of the farmhouse. A cement walk connected the end of the driveway to the front steps.

"Do you mind if I ask a few questions?" Holly queried.

"No," Blade replied, walking toward the porch.

"Why are you here?"

"I can't divulge the reason we came to Ohio," Blade said.

"The Soviets have renamed Ohio and call it Novgorod," Holly divulged, "but that's not what I meant. Why are you at our farm?"

"This was as good a place as any to acquire the information we need."

"About what?"

"Cincinnati. Have you visited the city?"

"Fairly frequently, particularly within the past year. Tim's trial was held in Cincinnati, and I was in the courtroom every day."

"Then you can provide a diagram of the streets and the Soviet installations."

"You plan to take on the Russians?"

Blade nodded. The house, he observed, was shrouded in gloom.

"Just the three of you?"

Blade nodded again.

"You're nuts."

"So we've been told."

Holly scrutinized the giant as they climbed the stairs and paused. "What do you hope to accomplish?"

"I can't say."

"I don't know why I should, but I'll do what I can to help you. I hate the damn Commies, and if you're going to give them a taste of their own medicine, then I'm all for it."

"Let's just say that they'll know we've been there."

Holly grinned. "Real men at last!"

Blade glanced at her. "Real men?"

"Most of the people have given up on the idea of opposing the Russians. There's the underground movement, but they're not very effective. They try to slip food to the needy, but they don't commit any violent acts because they're afraid of reprisals. It's nice to see men who aren't afraid, who aren't cowed by the Commies."

"You can't blame the people. Most, like your husband, probably have families, loved ones they wouldn't want to see harmed. Your Tim sounds like he was a . . .real man. The measure of manhood does not lie in a man's capacity for violence."

Holly folded her hands at her waist and gazed at him. "You're a strange one."

"Do you think any less of Tim even though he didn't rebel

openly?''

"No, I don't,'' Holly conceded.

"I rest my case.''

"Are there others like you where you come from?''

"Quite a few.''

"Too bad there aren't enough of you to overthrow the Russians.''

"One day, maybe,'' Blade said.

"I hope it happens during my lifetime. I want to see them ground into the dust. I want every last one of the mothers pushing up daisies,'' Holly stated harshly.

Blade grinned. "Maybe you should start a revolution yourself.''

"Maybe I will.''

The headlights were now several hundred yards south of the barn.

"Let's go in,'' Blade said, and opened the door for her. Once they were both in the hallway, he closed the door and positioned himself to the left, near the hinges.

"What do I do?'' Holly inquired.

"We wait to see who it is,'' Blade responded. "If they come to the door and knock, don't answer for at least a minute. We want them to think that they roused you out of bed.''

Holly reached out and flicked a metal button underneath the doorknob. "I locked it.''

"Thanks,'' Blade said. Why hadn't he thought of that? He suddenly realized he was feeling very fatigued, and he mentally chided himself for not having slept in over 24 hours. He'd attempted to rest early in the evening, after they had hidden the SEAL. Bothered by thoughts of Jenny and Gabe, and deeply upset at Geronimo's impending resignation from the Warriors, he'd tossed and turned in his seat, unable to doze off.

"I know that car,'' Holly stated, curtailing the giant's reverie. She was standing next to a narrow pane of glass on the right side of the jamb.

Blade peeked out, noting a rattling black sedan as the vehicle braked within a yard of the cement walk. "Who is it?''

"Gus Seuell. What does he want at this hour?"

"We'll know in a moment," Blade said. "Don't let him spot you."

Holly backed into the corner. "This is really weird. First you guys, now Gus. What gives tonight?"

"There's a full moon."

"Oh."

Blade heard a car door slam, then the sound of someone whistling. The tune was unfamiliar and erratic, rising in volume and tapering off repeatedly, as if the whistler wasn't concentrating on the song. Footsteps shuffled on the cement walk, and then the caller was on the front porch. Boots thudded up to the front door, and a fist pounded on the upper panel. Blade put his hands on the hilts of his Bowies.

"Open up!" a gruff voice barked. "This is Gus!" He knocked louder.

Holly went to move toward the doorknob, but Blade gestured with his left arm, stopping her.

"Open up, Holly!" Gus demanded. "I want to see you." A series of blows to the door accented his request. "Don't keep me waiting!"

"Now?" Holly whispered.

"Now."

Holly stepped to the door, released the lock, and pulled on the knob. "Gus," she said. "This is a surprise."

A gust of cool night air brushed Blade's face. He peered through the crack between the inner edge of the door and the jamb. Gus Seuell was a scarecrow of a man with a scraggly beard and a wispy mustache, dressed in a red flannel shirt and bib overalls.

"About time," Gus stated testily.

Blade's nostrils detected the odor of alcohol.

"Why are you here?" Holly asked, her arms folded across her chest.

"Can't you guess?" Gus responded.

"No. And I don't appreciate your behavior. You have no call to show up on my doorstep drunk, waking up my family at this ungodly hour.''

Gus craned his neck to gaze into the darkened hall. ''I don't see your family. All I see is you.''

''Why don't you come back after you've sobered up,'' Holly suggested.

''Like hell I will,'' Gus said, and seized her right forearm. Before she could break loose, he hauled her onto the porch and closed the door. ''We're going to talk.''

Shocked and indignant, Holly tried to wrest her arm free. ''Let go of me!''

''Not on your life, sweetheart,'' Gus said. ''I've got some words for you, and you're going to listen.''

''You're hurting me!''

Gus snickered. ''Ain't that a crying shame.'' He let go and leered at her. ''Why do you think I'm here?''

''I have no idea,'' Holly said, rubbing her forearm.

''Don't play the innocent with me,'' Gus stated, his breath reeking of whiskey.

''I don't know what you're talking about,'' Holly insisted.

''Sure you don't,'' Gus said.

''I don't,'' Holly repeated, reaching for the door.

Gus Seuell slapped her, a hard blow across the mouth, knocking her backwards. ''Don't touch that door!'' he hissed.

Holly pressed her right hand to her stinging mouth, tasting the salty tang of blood on her tongue.

''You're going to hear me out!'' Gus declared, stalking toward her.

Frightened by such cruel behavior in a man who previously had treated her with the utmost respect, Holly moved to the right, to the top step. ''Don't touch me!'' she warned.

Gus halted, his mouth twitching. ''All right. We'll play this your way.'' He took a pace nearer and she retreated to the cement walk.

''You'll never set foot on my property again,'' Holly said.

''That's what you think,'' Gus replied, and laughed. ''This isn't *your* property, you dumb broad. All the land belongs to the Ruskies, to the State. Diehards like your jerk of a husband

and you can't seem to accept the facts of life."

"I thought you liked Tim."

"Tim was a jackass. He believed he could resist the Commies. And he trusted me."

Holly forgot about her bleeding lips and lowered her hand as the implications of Seuell's comment dawned. "What do you mean?"

"Haven't you figured it out yet, missy?" Gus asked angrily, then tapped his chest. "I was the one who tipped the Ruskies to Tim's bin. I was the one who turned him in."

Holly was stupefied.

"That's right!" Gus gloated, savoring her shock. "I called the KGB and reported your husband's underground activities. I knew what would happen. Your idiot husband never suspected a thing."

"But why?" Holly blurted.

"Can't a smart woman like you figure it out? For years I've wanted you. For years I've dreamed about having you for myself. I came over here all the time not to see Tim, but to be close to you. I watched you cooking, and hanging the laundry, and feeding the cows and chickens." He paused, his expression softening. "You drove me crazy. I've never wanted anyone like I want you."

"You turned Tim in to the Russians," Holly said in a daze. "You were responsible for his execution."

"Damn straight I was. I knew I could never make a play for you while he was around, so I arranged to have him disposed of. I figured you'd open up to me after his death, but it's been six months and you treat me like I'm dirt."

Holly stared up at him, her eyes beginning to focus. "You killed Tim!"

"And I was paid in gold for doing it," Tim bragged. "The Russian commander himself thanked me for my patriotism." He tittered. "Can you imagine that? They paid me to get Tim out of the way."

"You bastard!" Holly exploded, springing at him, her nails raking at his eyes.

Gus shoved her from him, sending her sprawling onto the grass. He moved down the steps and stood at her feet. "You have this coming, bitch. I've waited long enough, and now I'm going to take what's mine. Everyone has dues to pay, woman. Everyone."

"How true," said a deep voice behind him.

Gus Seuell turned to find the biggest man he'd ever seen standing on the steps, looming above him like a colossus, blotting out the stars. "Who—?"

The colossus clamped his left hand on the back of Seuell's head, gripped Gus by the chin with his right, and wrenched his massive arms in a sharp, twisting motion. There was a pronounced snap and the betrayer went limp.

"Dear Lord!" Holly breathed.

Blade flung Gus Seuell's body contemptuously aside and looked at her. "Like the man said, everyone has dues to pay. He paid his."

A shiver ran along Holly's spine.

Chapter Nine

"Why the blazes do *I* have to do this?"

"You volunteered."

"That's funny. I don't recollect volunteering."

"I was going to have Geronimo do it, but he says you owe him one."

"That mangy Injun," Hickok muttered. He glared at Geronimo, who was standing 20 yards to the east.

Geronimo grinned and waved.

"There's no way he'll become a Tiller or a Hunter," Hickok declared.

"Why not?" Blade asked.

"He's too cussed ornery."

Blade wagged the Commando barrel at the asphalt. "Well, get to it." Hickok's AR-15 was slung over his left shoulder.

The gunman looked at the dusty roadway and frowned. "I'll get my duds dirty."

"Since when did you mind a little dirt?"

"It's not me I'm thinking of. It's my missus. Do you have any idea how hard it is to wash buckskins?"

"I'll be sure and tell her how devoted you are after we return to the Home," Blade said. "Now lay down."

Hickok eased onto his knees. "Why can't we just bushwhack the varmints?"

"We need their uniforms intact, not riddled with bullet holes," Blade noted, gazing at the woods lining the road.

"I feel like a blamed sittin' duck," Hickok groused, and lowered himself onto his stomach.

"All you have to do is lie there and pretend you're unconscious," Blade said. "We'll take care of the rest."

"I hope you know what you're doing."

"Look, we know the Russians patrol this stretch of road daily. This is the only road connecting Highway 127 to Dunlap, and this spot is ideal for our purposes. It's secluded, so we won't need to worry about witnesses."

Hickok placed his elbows on the asphalt and rested his chin in his hands. "How do you know we can trust that Eberle lady?"

"I trust my instincts."

"Oh, *now* I'm relieved."

"Holly was grateful to us for taking care of Gus Seuell. She offered to help us in any way she could. Thanks to her, we have a map of the city and we learned about this daily patrol."

"I hope the map she drew for you isn't a phony," Hickok commented. "I wouldn't want to think that Geronimo and I were wastin' our time burying all those flea-ridden mutts while you were in her kitchen sippin' hot coffee."

"Her dogs weren't flea-ridden."

"How would *you* know?"

Blade sighed and took several strides toward Geronimo. "We'll signal you when we see a vehicle."

"Thanks heaps. My missus would really be ticked if you let someone put tread marks on my buckskins."

"I hope they're on time," Blade stated.

"How'd Holly know about this patrol?"

"The underground movement her husband belonged to

keeps tabs on the Soviets,'' Blade said. ''A farmer living a
mile west of here is also part of the underground. He told Tim,
and Tim told her before he was executed.''

"Can't I hold onto my AR-15?''

"Nope. The patrol has to get right on top of you. You've
got your Pythons. What more do you want?''

"I want to hold Sherry in my arms and hear her tell me
how adorable I am. I want to take Ringo fishin' and watch
him get his line all tangled. I want to be at the Home, where
I don't have to watch my back every blasted minute of the
day. I want—''

"Sorry I asked,'' Blade said, cutting him off. He took a
pace, then paused and looked at the gunman.

"What's the matter?'' Hickok inquired.

"Is it my imagination, or are you as homesick as I am?''

"I am gettin' tired of all this gallivanting around the
country,'' Hickok replied. ''And I've been feelin' a bit
grumpy.''

"First me, then Geronimo, and now you,'' Blade said.
"Maybe all we really need is an extended vacation.''

"Sounds great, pard. Where do you want to go?''

"I don't know. I'll give it some thought.''

"Our wives will go for the notion. Sherry's always gripin'
that we never have enough time to ourselves,'' Hickok
mentioned. ''A holiday would do all of us a world of good.
The wives can cook us some grub and set up a picnic
somewhere and watch the young'uns while we kick back and
shoot the breeze.''

Blade glanced at the gunfighter. ''That's your idea of a
vacation?''

"Yep. What's wrong with it?''

"Oh, nothing. But I want to be there when you tell Sherry.''

Geronimo suddenly whistled and waved his right arm.

"Here they come,'' Blade said. ''Now remember my
instructions. I don't want bullet holes in their uniforms.''

"Piece of cake.''

Blade hurried to Geronimo's side. ''What did you see?''

"There," Geronimo said, pointing.

A green vehicle was cresting a low hill 300 yards to the east.

"Think it's the Soviets?" Geronimo queried.

"We'll soon know," Blade said, and jogged back toward Hickok. Ten yards from the gunman, he veered to the left and took cover in the underbrush.

Geronimo stayed right beside him. "What's Nathan doing?" he asked as he crouched down.

Blade gazed at the road.

Hickok was lying on his right side, his head propped on his right arm, twirling a Colt Python in his left hand and humming.

"Lie down!" Blade ordered.

The Family's supreme gunman sighed and flattened. He drew his right Python, then tucked them both under his chest, screening the Magnums from view. He angled his body slightly so his back was to the east.

"This will never work," Geronimo remarked.

Blade trained his eyes eastward. "Why not?"

"They won't stop. The Russians will take one look at Hickok and run him over."

"Wishful thinking."

The sound of an engine reached their ears.

"Hey," Geronimo declared, as if an idea had just occurred to him.

"What?"

"They really might not stop," Geronimo stated, his tone reflecting his worry. "Or they might pump a few rounds into him instead of checking him out. What do we do then?"

"If they don't slow down, or if one of them so much as lifts a weapon, we waste them."

"Good," Geronimo said, clearly relieved. "Not that I care, of course."

"Of course."

The growl of the motor grew louder, and a jeep filled with Soviet soldiers appeared 70 yards to the east.

Blade fingered the Commando's trigger. The sight of the familiar brown uniforms reminded him of the run he'd taken to Philadelphia with Sundance and Bertha. They'd been lucky to escape with their lives. The Russians were a perennial threat to the Family and the Freedom Federation. Perhaps Holly Eberle had the right idea. Perhaps the Freedom Federation should give serious consideration to invading Soviet territory and driving the Communists into the Atlantic Ocean.

Geronimo pressed the SAR stock to his right shoulder and sighted on the vehicle.

The jeep was 40 yards from Hickok's prone form when the driver braked. Seconds later the door on the passenger side opened and three Soviet soldiers climbed out, each one armed with an AK-47. They engaged in a brief discussion, with the tallest gesturing repeatedly at the figure blocking their path. Finally they advanced, spreading out, the tallest moving down the center of the road flanked by his companions. The jeep stayed where it was, the engine idling, the driver leaning forward to peer out the windshield.

Blade glanced at Geromino and nodded at the jeep.

Geronimo melted into the undergrowth.

The trio of troopers halted 15 yards from Hickok and the tallest shouted a few words in Russian, then switched to English. "You there! Stand up!"

Hickok did not budge.

"Did you hear me? Stand up!" the tallest soldier instructed warily.

Hickok remained motionless.

Cautiously, their AK-47s trained on the buckskin-clad form, the three troopers walked forward slowly. Two yards away they stopped again.

"If this is a trick, you will live to regret it!" the tallest soldier declared. "Roll over so we can see your hands!"

Hickok was like a rock.

"You have been warned," the tallest soldier said, and stepped up to the gunman and rammed the AK-47 barrel into Hickok's back.

Still Hickok did not move.

The tallest trooper looked at his comrades, both of whom

edged closer.

Blade watched as the tallest soldier reached for Hickok's right shoulder. He rose and started toward the road, intending to burst from cover and take the Soviets unawares. Capturing four prisoners increased the likelihood that one of the Russians would know something about the Soviet superweapon. He hoped to interrogate all four, but his hopes were dashed by, of all things, a tangled clump of weeds. As he darted into the open his right combat boot caught on the clump and he tripped, pitching onto his knees, using the Commando stock to catch himself,—but the damage was already done. The muted thud of his knees striking the earth alerted the four Russians.

The soldiers spun, swinging their AK-47s around.

Blade saw the barrels swiveling in his direction and tensed, expecting to feel searing agony as dozens of rounds perforated his torso. In the fleeting instant before the troopers went to squeeze the triggers on their AK-47, he thought of Jenny and Gabe.

His vision of his death, however, was premature.

Even as the soldiers were turning, the man who was recognized by the Family as the greatest gunfighter in the 105-year history of their survivalist group, the man who was renowned in the Freedom Federation for his lightning speed and unerring accuracy, was flipping onto his back, his arms sweeping up and out, the Colt Pythons gleaming in the late afternoon sun. Three shots boomed as one.

The soldiers never knew what hit them. One moment they were about to slay a giant in a black leather vest, and the next blackness engulfed them as a hollow-point slug passed completely through their head from back to front, exploding their foreheads outward in a spray of flesh, blood, and brains. All three sprawled to the asphalt, the AK-47s falling from their limp fingers.

Blade surged erect and looked at the jeep.

Geronimo had the driver's door wide, and was covering the soldier behind the wheel with his SAR.

"Like I said, pard. A piece of cake."

Blade turned.

Hickok was already erect, inspecting the troopers to insure they were lifeless.

"Thanks," Blade stated. "Jenny was almost a widow."

"I'd do the same for any other klutz."

Blade unslung the AR-15. "Here. Haul the bodies into the brush while I talk to the driver."

Hickok came over, holstered his left colt, and took the rifle. "Why am I doing all the heavy work on this run?"

"You can use the exercise."

"How do you figure that?"

"You were the one who couldn't outrun an overfed pack of farm dogs," Blade remarked, and headed for the jeep.

"*Somebody* around here definitely needs a vacation," Hickok muttered.

Blade ignored the gunman and hurried to the vehicle. "At least we got one," he commented to Geronimo.

"What was that move you pulled?" Geronimo inquired. "Were you trying to make them laugh so hard they'd drop their weapons?"

"Go help Hickok," Blade stated. "After the bodies are concealed, strip off the uniforms. I'll keep an eye on our friend." He pointed the Commando at the driver.

"I am not your friend, pig!" the soldier snapped. He was in his thirties, a husky trooper with sandy hair and blue eyes. His pudgy features were set defiantly, and his double chin quivered as he tried to suppress his rage at the deaths of his comrades.

"Oink," Geronimo said, and jogged toward Hickok.

"Put the jeep in park and raise your hands," Blade commanded.

The trooper glowered at the giant. "You will pay for what you have done, bastard!"

"Do it or die," Blade stated grimly.

His lips curling in a scowl, the pudgy Russian stared at the Commando for a second, then complied.

"What's your name?" Blade asked.

"Vsevolod Fedorov."

"How about if I just call you Fred?"

"Screw you, shithead."

Blade took a step nearer and smacked the Commando barrel against the trooper's nose.

Fedorov screeched and cupped his hands over his nostrils. "Damn you! You broke it!" he cried.

"Not yet," Blade responded, "but I will if you give me any more lip. Now raise those hands!"

Hesitantly, tears of frustration welling in his eyes, his nose throbbing in anguish, Fedorov slowly elevated his arms.

"That's better. Are you based in Cincinnati?"

Fedorov gazed straight ahead, deliberately averting his eyes. His lips twitched, but he refused to answer.

Blade sighed and touched the barrel to the soldier's left cheek. "I don't have time to play games with you. If you won't tell me what I want to know, I'll kill you now and find another Russian trooper who will."

Fedorov looked at the Warrior with hatred in his eyes. "Who are you kidding? You'll kill me anyway, whether I talk or not. So shoot me and get it over with!"

"If you cooperate, I won't kill you."

"Ha! I don't believe you."

Blade shrugged. "Suit yourself. I've given you my word. but if you want to die needlessly, that's your business."

"I'm not a traitor."

"Of course you're not. You're a loyal Communist and you believe in every word of The Communist Manifesto."

Fedorov's forehead furrowed.

"You're ready to die for Mother Russia, the country you were born and reared in," Blade went on, knowing full well that his statements were inaccurate. During the course of the Family's previous dealings with the Soviets, the Warriors had learned crucial details concerning the Russian invasion of America.

The Soviet Union had successfully occupied a section of the

eastern United States during the war, but their drive in the west, a push through Alaska and western Canada spearheaded by armored divisions, was stopped cold in British Columbia by the harshest winter weather in centuries. The Russians consolidated their iron grip on the territory they controlled in the eastern U.S., but a severe shortage of armaments, ammunition, general supplies, and replacement personnel prevented them from penetrating past the Mississippi River or expanding into the deep South. For 70 years they maintained communications with the Motherland. The commanders of the Russian occupation forces pleaded for more troops, more tanks, and more supplies. Except for infrequent shipments, their pleas were largely ignored.

The Soviet Union was having problems of its own. Russia's industrial capacity had been reduced to almost nil by the American nuclear strikes, and the U.S.S.R. rapidly depleted its natural resources. To compound the Communists' problem, that which they feared most happened; the ethnic groups they had oppressed for scores of years finally saw their chance and rebelled. The Tartars and the Balts, the Mordivians and the Udmurts, and every other group the Communist Party had tryannized rose up against their former masters.

To their dismay, the Russian forces in America became stranded, trapped in the very country they had sought to conquer. All broadcasts and cryptographic contact with the Soviet Union inexplicably ceased. A few ships and planes were sent to investigate and never returned. Thrown on their own resources, with their provisions low and their morale even lower, the Russian commanders established a dictatorial system as ruthless as Stalin's. Slave-labor camps were set up, summary executions were conducted routinely, and an American branch of the KGB went into operation. All industries still operational were rechanneled for Soviet purposes. The section of America under Communist rule became a carbon copy of the Motherland.

The Russians were able to manufacture the ammunition they

required for their AK-47s and other small arms. Their
helicopter fleet was their primary military focus; every
available plant capable of being modified to produce helicopter
parts was put into service. Their efforts to keep their jets in
the air, however, met with failure. They lacked the resources
and facilities to construct the specialized jet parts, and
eventually their Air Force consisted solely of helicopters.

Another major problem involved their shortage of
replacement personnel. They realized attrition would gradually
reduce their force to undesirable levels unless drastic measures
were taken. So a system of modified racial breeding was
instituted, in which selected American women were forcibly
impregnated and compelled to give birth. The children were
then turned over to the State and raised in Russian-regulated
dormitories, where they were subjected to intensive
indoctrination. Communism was extolled, Russian history and
values were inculcated, and every aspect of the education and
training the orphans received was designed to create soldiers
and citizens as loyal as they would have been had they been
reared in the U.S.S.R.

Blade knew all of this, and the look of confusion on
Fedorov's face almost made him laugh. "I admire a man
willing to die for a cause he believes in. I'm sure your parents
will be proud of you."

"I don't have any parents," Fedorov said.

"No? Then I'd imagine your sergeant and your commanding
officer will be equally pleased by your loyalty," Blade said.
"Of course, they'll never know how brave you were." He
lowered his chin and sighted on the soldier's left ear.

Vsevolod Fedorov was chewing on his lower lip. He glanced
at the Commando barrel and gulped.

"So long," Blade said, tightening his grip.

"Hold it!" Fedorov blurted. "Don't shoot!"

Blade straightened. "Why shouldn't I?"

"Look, mister, I don't want to die. I've never been to
Russia. I was raised at a State School, and I was told my
parents died shortly after I was born. My sergeant is a son

of a bitch, and my commanding officer couldn't care less about my welfare.''

"So you'll cooperate in exchange for your life?"

Fedorov grinned weakly. ''What do you want to know?''

Chapter Ten

"This wasn't part of the deal."

"Just drive."

"All I agreed to do was answer your questions," Fedorov complained. "You never said anything about bringing you to Cincinnati."

"Think of yourself as our chaperon," Blade suggested.

"I'll wind up in front of a firing squad for this," Fedorov said.

"Only if we're caught," Blade noted. "You'd better hope we're not."

Federov turned the steering wheel to negotiate a curve. "I would have been better off if *you* shot me," he mumbled.

"That can always be arranged, cow-chip," Hickok mentioned from his seat behind the Russian. "I'm gettin' tired of hearin' you flap your gums." He looked down at himself. "And I feel downright naked without my buckskins."

"You smell better in a Soviet uniform," Geronimo remarked, sitting in the cramped back seat next to the gunman.

"What's that crack supposed to mean?" Hickok asked.

"After a heavy rain you always smell like a doe in heat," Geronimo mentioned casually.

"I do not."

"Stand outside for a while the next time it rains, then go in your cabin and take a whiff. I'm surprised Sherry hasn't told you about the odor."

"You're makin' this up to get my goat," Hickok declared.

"I didn't know you owned one."

Fedorov glanced at the giant beside him. "Are you guys escapees from a State Mental Health Ward?"

Blade gazed at the trooper. "No. Where would you ever get an idea like that?"

"Nowhere," Fedorov said, and concentrated on his driving.

The head Warrior grinned as he stared through the windshield at the street ahead. They were winding through a residential neighborhood two miles northwest of downtown Cincinnati, and on both sides were modest frame or brick homes, most in dire need of a fresh coat of paint or repair. Most driveways were empty, although a few antique automobiles were in evidence in the drives of the infrequently encountered residences which had been fully restored. Children played in yards or on the sidewalks, while the adults lounged on porches or congregated for conversations at the street corners. Most of the adults gave the jeep an openly hostile stare, but the youngsters, involved with their playing, scarcely noticed.

"This isn't what I expected," Blade commented.

"What did you expect?" Fedorov queried.

Blade shrugged. "Bars on every window. Armed soldiers patrolling every road. Checkpoints at every intersection."

"There are checkpoints at the major entry points into the city," Fedorov said. "But there aren't enough soldiers to cover every secondary road and side street. If we're lucky, we'll reach our destination without being spotted by a patrol."

"What's with all these folks?" Hickok asked. "Why are they allowed to roam free?"

"They can't go anywhere," Fedorov responded. "Most of them don't own cars, and they wouldn't get very far outside the city on foot. Our helicopters would nail them if our road patrols didn't."

"We got through," Hickok mentioned.

"You were lucky."

"We call it skill," Geronimo interjected.

"These people don't have your luck or your skill," Fedorov said. "They're stuck here for the rest of their miserable lives."

"Do they own these homes?" Blade questioned.

"Of course not. The State owns everything. As long as they behave, the State allows them to live in a designated house. A lot of them like to think the home they live in is theirs, but they're just kidding themselves."

Blade stared at the deceptively tranquil setting, pondering. Apparently the Russian subjugation of the urban centers was thorough and stifling, in contrast to the Soviets' lax attitude toward the rural areas. The Russians tended to concentrate their activities in the cities, which explained their urban regimentation. And the strategy made sense. The cities were the hubs of commerce and culture; anyone who dominated the urban centers held the upper hand over the outlying areas. If nothing else, the Russians were systemical and logical in their methods.

Fedorov came to an intersection and took a right.

"How much farther?" Blade inquired.

"About a mile and a half," Fedorov answered.

"Tell me again about the installation," Blade directed.

"I've already gone over it twice," Fedorov groused.

"Humor me."

The soldier sighed, then tensed when a car approached from the opposite direction. He relaxed once he perceived the brown sedan was not a military vehicle. "All the information I've heard, you understand, is secondhand. Friends of mine who were assigned as perimeter guards told me about this place."

"Construction began about a year ago?"

"Yeah. There used to be a school at the same site, some

kind of religious school I believe. The name of the place was the College of Mount Something-or-Other, and it was abandoned during World War Three. Then about a year ago construction crews arrived there, and they started repairing the damaged buildings and erecting new ones. A huge wall was built, enclosing everything. Barbed wire was strung up on top of the walls. There must be hundreds of people working there, scientists and what not, but the projects they're working on are hush-hush. The guards stay in a barracks near the front gate. No one can get on the premises without a special pass, and certain buildings are off limits except for those with a Top Secret clearance.''

''Sounds like what we're looking for,' Geronimo said.

''I heard that the place is run by the Ministry of Defense,'' Fedorov divulged. ''But that wouldn't explain all the scientists unless the Ministry of Science is working with the Ministry of Defense.''

''Does that ever happen?'' Blade questioned.

''All the time. The military runs the show.''

They continued in silence for 15 minutes, with Fedorov taking the least-frequented streets and back roads, traversing several steep hills as they wound ever lower toward the Ohio River. The city of Cincinnati was arranged in a succession of gradual terraces. The residential neighborhoods were largely concentrated on the steep hills, some of which rose over 450 feet above the Ohio River. Comprising the second level was the former business district, where State-managed shops now offered limited selections for the ''liberated working class,'' as Fedorov described the shabbily dressed customers for the benefit of the Warriors. On the lowest level, approximately 60 feet above the low-water mark of the Ohio River, was the manufacturing section of the metropolis.

Blade gazed at the meandering, murky Ohio, and observed a half-dozen boats and one ship, a freighter, plying the waters of the river. According to the Atlas in the SEAL, Cincinnati had served as a transportation hub for the United States prior to the nuclear exchange, and the Soviets were likewise utilizing the city's unique geographic characteristics wisely. While the Ohio River constituted a natural boundary to the south, two other rivers were also of importance, the Little Miami to the east and the Great Miami to the west. Perhaps, Blade speculated, the city's prominence as a transportation center accounted for the fact the Russians had not nuked it.

"Are we getting close?" Blade queried impatiently.

"Close," Fedorov assured him.

Blade twisted in his seat, feeling extremely uncomfortable in the tight-fitting Russian uniform taken from the tallest trooper. The clothes barely fit; the sleeves rode two inches above his wrists, the lower hem of the pants covered the top inch of his combat boots, and the pants threatened to split at the seam with every breath he took. His vest and fatigue pants were bundled under the seat. The Commando rested on his lap, while his Bowies were tucked underneath his shirt, supported by the narrow belt worn by all Soviet troopers. He stared to the west at the setting sun, pleased that twilight was rapidly descending.

"What do you want me to do when we get there?" Fedorov asked.

"Can we drive past the installation without attracting attention?"

"Sure. Delhi Road goes right past the front wall."

"Then do it."

Fedorov took a left, then a right, and ultimately turned onto Delhi Road. He flicked on the headlights.

More vehicles were in evidence, dozens of them traveling in both directions. Very few were civilian automobiles.

Hickok leaned forward and placed the AR-15 barrel behind Fedorov's right ear. "One false move, you coyote, and I'll ventilate your noggin."

Fedorov licked his thick lips and wiped the palm of his left hand on his shirt. "What kind of idiot do you take me for?"

"The cream of the crop."

Fedorov tried to swivel his head to look at the gunman, but

the AR-15 barrel jammed into his ear. "I've helped you so far."

"So far," Hickok conceded.

"Then why not take that gun away from my ear?"

"Can't. The front sight has grown real attached to your earlobe."

"You're weird. Has anyone ever told you that?"

"Practically everyone," Geronimo chimed in. "But it's difficult to impress a point on someone who has the cranial capacity of marble."

"You're both weird," Fedorov declared.

Hickok glanced at Geronimo. "Cranial capacity? Have you been readin' Plato's books again?"

"I don't need to read Plato's books. I can recognize a rock formation when I see one."

Fedorov cleared his throat and looked at Blade. "Do you mind if I ask you a question?"

"What?"

"Are these two guys always like this?"

Blade nodded.

"I don't see how you put up with it," Fedorov commented.

"I look at it as good practice."

"Practice?"

"I have a three-year-old."

Fedorov nodded. "I see."

"I think we've just been insulted," Hickok said.

"I *know* we've just been insulted," Geronimo amended.

They continued to the west and came to an intersection, crossing Anderson Ferry Road and proceeding another quarter of a mile.

Hickok glanced out his window, his blue eyes widening slightly. "What the dickens is that!" he exclaimed.

"That's the installation," Fedorov said.

Blade bent down and stared to the left, marveling at the size of the facility, impressed by the magnitude of every structure. The outer stone walls were 40 feet high and crowned with another six feet of thorny barbed wire. Positioned on the rim of the wall at 20-foot intervals were huge spotlights, all of which were already on. Rearing above the wall on the far side were enormous buildings, architectural behemoths fabricated from stone and glass, startlingly futuristic and incongruous in the otherwise run down and neglected metropolis. The centerpiece of the mysterious installation was a tremendous silver spire capped by a crystal globe 30 feet in diameter. Blade estimated the spire towered 500 feet in the air.

"And you say you don't know the name of this facility?" Geronimo asked the soldier skeptically.

"I don't know if it has a name," Fedorov answered. "Everyone calls it the L.R.F."

"What does L.R.F. stand for?" Geronimo probed.

"Like I told your leader here, I don't know."

"How in the blazes are we going to get in there?" Hickok inquired. "Sprout wings and fly over the wall?"

"I do know the name of the spire," Fedorov mentioned.

"You do?" Blade responded. "What is it called?"

"Lenin's Needle."

Hickok snorted. "And you call us weird?"

"Hey, I didn't name the spire. I only know that's what it's called," Fedorov said. "It's not healthy to go around asking a whole lot of questions about anything, let alone a restricted facility like L.R.F."

"You must have heard rumors," Blade commented.

"I heard the place is being used to shoot down planes," Fedorov said. "But that's ridiculous. No one has seen an enemy plane over Cincinnati in ages." He paused and looked at Lenin's Needle. "Of course, that might explain the red light . . ." he began, then stopped as the giant abruptly gripped his right shoulder.

"A red light?" Blade said.

"You're hurting me," Fedorov declared, trying to slide his shoulder from under the giant's brawny hand.

Blade increased the pressure. "What red light are you talking about?" he queried intensely.

"Every now and then a bright red light shoots out of the spire," Fedorov explained. "On a clear day or night the light can be seen for miles."

Blade released his hold and studied Lenin's Needle, perplexed. What type of weapon could be housed in such an edifice? What was the significance of the crystal globe? for the Soviets to invest such a staggering sum in so mammoth a facility indicated they were supremely confident in the ultimate success of the project—whatever it was.

The jeep was drawing abreast of the front entrance.

"Look at the size of the gate!" Hickok said.

The front entrance to the installation was as impressive as the rest of the engineering. A 30-foot-tall metal gate, latticed with horizontal and vertical bars six inches thick, was the sole means of entry. Two dozens soldiers stood at attention outside the open gate while a pair of officers examined the identification cards of everyone passing inside. A short, wide drive, 20 feet in length, connected Delhi Road to the L.R.F.

Fedorov gazed at the massive portal as he drove. "They keep the gate open during the day, but it's locked up tight as a drum at night. The day shift is probably heading home, and they'll be closing the gate soon."

Blade craned his neck for a glimpse of the interior, but all he could distinguish were the outlines of several of the gigantic structures. The base of the spire, located in the middle of the sprawling compound, was not visible from the road. He pursed his lips, annoyed. Hickok was right. How *were* they going to get in there? The walls were too high to scale, and even if they could, there was no way they could evade all those spotlights and clamber over the bared wire undetected. Scaling the gate, with so many guards on the premises, was impractical. Clandestine infiltration was their best bet. But how?

They were less than two car lengths to the east of the entrance when an unexpected development provided an unwanted solution to their problem.

"Look out!" Geronimo suddenly cried, pointing straight

ahead.

Fedorov, fascinated by the monstrous gate and walls, had neglected to keep his eyes on the road. He swung around to find a panel truck had braked not 15 feet away, and he slammed on the jeep's brakes in a frantic bid to avoid a collision. The jeep slewed to the left, slowing rapidly, its tires squealing.

Blade clutched the dashboard. For a moment he thought they would miss the truck, but seconds later the front fender slammed into the rear of the bronze-colored panel truck. There was a loud crunch and a crash as the front headlight on the driver's side was smashed by the impact, then the tinkling of broken glass falling to the asphalt.

"No!" Fedorov wailed. "No! No! No!"

All the vehicles behind the jeep had stopped, and those in the other lane were slowing so the occupants could gawk.

"We must get out of here!" Federov cried.

"Stay calm," Blade stated. "Don't lose your head."

The driver of the panel truck hopped out and stalked toward their jeep, his fists clenched at his sides. A burly man, he wore a blue flannel shirt and brown pants.

"That guy looks like he sat on a broom handle," Hickok quipped.

"What do I do?" Fedorov asked, panic-stricken.

"Calm down," Blade reiterated in a quiet tone.

"You don't understand . . ." Fedorov started to respond.

The driver of the panel truck reached the rear corner and glared at the dent in his vehicle. He shook his right fist at Fedorov. "Where did you learn to drive? New Jersey?"

"We're dead," Fedorov declared.

"What are you talking about?" Blade responded. "You're a soldier. Get out and talk to him, but just remember we'll have you covered. There's no reason to get all bent out of shape."

"I think there is, pard," Hickok commented, and jerked his left thumb toward the gate.

Blade looked at the front entrance to the L.R.F. and felt the hair on the nape of his neck tingle.

An officer and six troopers were heading their way!

Chapter Eleven

"What am I going to do?" Fedorov whimpered, gaping at the approaching officer, a lieutenant.

"Don't overreact," Blade cautioned. "We can bluff our way out of this mess."

"They'll kill me if they find out I was helping you," Fedorov said.

"They won't find out," Blade assured the Russian.

"Yes, they will," Fedorov disagreed. "You don't know them like I do."

The lieutenant and the six soldiers were 12 feet distant.

"I'm getting out of here!" Fedorov unexpectedly cried, and shifted into reverse. He tramped on the accelerator, sending the jeep flying backwards to crash into a brown automobile, then wrenched on the wheel and tried to maneuver into the opposite lane, an impossible feat because the other lane was crammed with vehicles.

"What the hell are you doing?" tthe driver of the panel truck shouted.

"Don't!" Blade snapped. "We're already boxed in. You're only making it worse."

Fedorov wasn't about to let up. He pounded on the horn, frantically striving to clear the obstructing traffic.

The detail from the gate halted, and the officer cupped his hand around his mouth. "You there! What do you think you're doing! Do not move your vehicle!"

"We're in for trouble now," Geronimo predicted.

Blade was furious. Fedorov's stupidity was attracting precisely the attention he wanted to avoid at all costs. "Quit using the horn!" he growled.

"I don't want to die!" Fedorov blubbered, his fleshy features trembling.

The driver of the panel truck stepped over to their jeep and kicked the grill. "Turn it off and step out here!"

"I figure we should make a break for it," Hickok advised, holding the AR-15 in his lap. His prized Pythons were concealed under his uniform shirt, the barrels held fast by his belt, with the pearl grips reversed. To draw he first had to unbutton the shirt and reach in, and he disliked the delay the unbuttoning would cause. In an emergency he wanted to be able to reach his Pythons as quickly as possible, and by his reckoning the current situation qualified as the genuine article.

"For once I agree with Hickok," Geronimo concurred.

The lieutenant and the six soldiers were on the far side of the opposing lane of traffic, blocked by a truck and a car that were touching bumper to bumper. Gesticulating and barking orders, the officer was attempting to get them to separate.

"This sucks!" Fedorov declared, and yanked on the door handle.

Blade lunged, trying to restrain the trooper, his left hand catching hold of Fedorov's right wrist.

"Let go of me!" Fedorov yelled, tugging and thrashing, his left leg and arm outside the jeep.

"What is happening?" the officer demanded. "Private! Answer me!"

Fedorov glanced at the officer. "Comrade Lieutenant, help

ne! These men are enemies of the State! They've been holding ne prisoner!''

"This is gettin' ridiculous," Hickok said, and jabbed the AR-15 into Fedorov's ribs and squeezed the trigger.

The burst tore Fedorov from Blade's grasp and flung him against the car in the opposite lane, his chest riddled, oozing blood, his face a mask of astonishment. His lips twitched feebly and he slumped to the asphalt.

Hickok was already in motion, firing as he climbed from the jeep, sending a round into the stunned lieutenant's forehead and catapulting the officer backwards into two troopers. He shot a soldier who was endeavoring to unlimber an AK-47, then a private who looked like he was trying to catch flies with his mouth.

"What the hell!" the driver of the panel truck blurted out, then dove for the ground when a giant and another guy popped from the jeep that had hit his truck.

Blade saw the Russians near the gate start toward Delhi Road. He raised the Commando and cut loose, swinging the weapon in a tight arc, and he was gratified to see five of the soldiers go down. The Commando Arms Carbine was a devasting piece of firepower; three feet in length, only eight pounds in weight, with a fully automatic capability thanks to he Family Gunsmiths. Using its 90-round magazine of 45-caliber ammunition, the commando was lightweight, versatile, and supremely deadly.

The driver's door on a truck 30 feet to the east opened, and a soldier materialized with a pistol in his right hand.

Geronimo shot him through the chest.

The guards at the gate were hitting the dirt. Screams arose from women in several of the vehicles. The four remaining soldiers who had accompanied the lieutenant ducked behind the car in the other lane.

For several seconds the pressure was off the Warriors.

"Which way, pard?" Hickok asked, swiveling from right to left, trying to cover every direction at once.

Blade backed toward the sidewalk. The decision was already

made for him. They were entirely hemmed in by vehicles on three sides. Attempting to assualt the installation would be virtual suicide. Their sole avenue of escape lay to the north. A row of dilapidated buildings bordered Delhi Road on the north side, most with peeling paint and dirty windows, all of them apparently vacant. Which figured. The Soviets wouldn't want anyone living or working in close proximity to their top-secret facility where their activities could be monitored. "This way!" he shouted.

Geronimo dashed to Blade's side.

A trooper appeared above the hood of the car, an AK-47 pressed to his shoulder.

Hickok was faster, the AR-15 chattering instantly, and the trooper screeched and fell from view. The gunman whirled and clambered swiftly over the jeep's hood, then back pedaled to his friends. "Let's skedaddle," he declared.

"On me," Blade directed, sprinting to the west, surprised to discover scattered pedestrians on the sidewalk, all of whom frantically endeavored to flee out of his path. He could hear Geronimo and Hickok pounding on his heels, and then a new sound, the harsh thundering of AK-47s.

A large window in a deserted store to their rear shattered.

"They're gettin' our range!" Hickok exclaimed, halting and pivoting and firing from the hip.

Two Russian soldiers near the car died on their feet.

Hickok resumed his flight, looking at the L.R.F. and observing a score of soldiers rushing through the gate. "Reinforcements are comin'!" he yelled.

Blade and Geronimo slowed, covering the gunman while he caught up.

"This is gettin' serious," Hickok cracked.

"What was your first clue?" Geronimo asked.

Blade glanced to the west and spied an alley 15 feet distant. "Move!" he ordered, sprinting forward, scarcely noticing the rusted, decrepit trash cans littering the sidewalk as he darted into the mouth of the alley. His boots crunched on refuse and a stench assailed his nostrils. Mounds of moldy garbage lined the walls.

"P.U.!" Hickok said. "Why do you always pick places that smell like the butt end of a cow with the runs?"

"Damn!" Blade snapped.

"I knew this would happen," Geronimo stated.

A ten-foot-high brick wall blocked their passage.

Blade slung the Commando over his right arm and cupped his hands. "Let's go. Hickok first."

The gunman placed his right boot on Blade's hands. "Don't get carried away," he said, slinging the AR-15 over his left shoulder.

Blade's arms surged upward, and Hickok sailed overhead. The gunfighter cleared the top of the wall with a yard to spare and descended on the far side. A veritable din ensued, a metallic clanging and clashing intermixed with muffled exclamations. "Hickok are you all right?" Blade queried anxiously.

"Fine," came the angry reply.

"What happened?"

"I landed in a blamed trash can."

Geronimo smirked. "All the grace of a rhino," he commented, and looked over his shoulder. Loud voices emanated from the mouth of the alley, but no one was in sight. The Soviets were being cautious.

"Your turn," Blade said.

"How many points do I make if I clobber Hickok?" Geronimo asked as he slipped his left foot into Blade's hands.

Blade hurled Geronimo toward the lip of the wall.

"Down here!" someone near the street bellowed.

Time for a deterrent. Blade faced Delhi, unslung the Commando, and let off a short burst to discourage their pursuers. He spun and vaulted upward, the Commando in his left hand, easily taking hold of the rim of the wall with his right hand and employing his left elbow as a brace. The next moment he was up and over and dropping to the sidewalk beyond, landing between his fellow Warriors.

Geronimo stood to the right, scrutinizing the deserted street before them. The gathering nightfall blanketed the structures.

Hickok was busily removing bits and pieces of revolting gunk from his clothing. At his feet was an overturned trash can dotted with rust holes. "What's with all the blasted garbage?" he wanted to know.

"Maybe this whole area was abandoned before the L.R.F. was built," Blade speculated, surveying the street. "Maybe there are homeless people in Cincinnati who are using these vacant buildings for shelter."

"I doubt the Commies would let folks wander around the city," Hickok said, scrunching up his nose as he picked a gooey green glob from his uniform shirt.

"The Russians can't be everywhere at once. And I doubt they rate apprehending homeless people as a very high priority."

"Where to now?" Geronimo inquired. "Every Soviet soldier in the city will be after us."

Blade jogged to the left, bearing to the east, reversing direction to confound the enemy.

"Do you have a plan?" Geronimo asked, staying on the giant's right.

"Yeah. It's called staying alive."

"You'd best do better than that," Hickok said, a yard to their rear. "This is terrible."

"Since when have you ever been worried about handling several thousand Russian soldiers?" Geronimo responded.

"It's not the Commies who worry me," Hickok declared. "It's our wives."

"Our wives?"

"Yep. They'll tan our hides for losin' our duds."

They covered 50 yards and reached the front of an enormous dingy building.

Blade abruptly swerved to the right and bounded up a flight of cracked and pitted cement stairs to the wooden door.

"What gives, pard?" Hickok questioned. "I don't much

like the notion of being cornered indoors."

"We'll cut through here. This building should front Delhi Road. If the Spirit smiles on us, we should come out behind the Russians."

Geronimo looked at the alley. "Speaking of the Russians, where are they?"

"They probably had to regroup," Blade said. "They'll be coming over the wall any second." He gripped the doorknob and pulled, and to his delight the door swung out. "Stay close to me," he advised, and plunged into the gloomy recesses of the brownstone.

Geronimo went in next.

Hickok hesitated for a last glimpse of the alley, and he saw several soldiers jumping to the sidewalk as he eased the door shut. The inside of the building was damp and musty.

"Let's go," Blade stated, standing eight feet off, his immense form an indistinct inky shadow.

"I need someone to hold my hand," Hickok joked.

"Why do you think Sherry married you?" Geromino replied sarcastically.

"The woman has excellent taste."

"In food."

The Warriors advanced tentatively, feeling their way in the darkness, occasionally encountering rickety furniture and dangling spider webs.

"I just had a thought," Hickok whispered.

"There's a first," Geronimo said.

"I'm serious, pard. What if there are mutants in here?"

"They'll pick up your scent and head for the hills."

"I don't smell that bad."

"A horny skunk would be in seventh heaven."

They came to a junction and Blade led them to the left, along a narrow corridor. Rustling and squeaking noises fluttered in the air.

"This dump is spooky," Hickok commented.

In 20 yards they came to another intersection, and as they took a right they walked into a wall of sticky cobwebs.

"Yuck," Hickok said, swiping at the invisible strands.

"I can see a faint light at the end of the hall," Blade mentioned.

"Lead on," Geronimo stated.

Blade moved toward the vague illumination, batting cobwebs aside with every stride. "This might be our way out."

"None too soon," Hickok said. He took three steps on the heels of the others, then froze when something the size of his hand, something wiggling and heavy, plummeted out of the blackness overhead and landed in his hair.

Chapter Twelve

Blade sidled up to the door, the Commando in his right hand, clasped the smooth doorknob, and placed his left ear to the panel. The upper and lower edges of the door were outlined in a pale glow. Beyond were the sounds of upraised voices, honking vehicles, and the tramping of boots on the pavement. He tested the knob to verify the door was unlocked, and circumspectly eased the door open several inches.

Delhi Road was swirling with activity. The traffic jam was worse than before; evidently the officers on the scene were not permitting any of the vehicles to budge. Military uniforms were everywhere, with a heavy concentration in the proximity of the jeep. The colossal front gate hung open, and three rows of soldiers stood at attention near the entrance. People lined the sidewalks, watching the soldiers bustling to and fro. An ambulance was parked in the drive to the L.R.F., its red lights flashing. Stars sparkled in the heavens.

"We'll mingle with the crowd," Blade whispered over his left shoulder. "Then head for the downtown area."

"We're right behind you," Geronimo assured him.

Blade jerked the door open. A sign was attached to the wall to his right, within a foot of the jamb, its black lettering illuminated by the combined glare of the numerous headlights and spotlights.

WARNING: THIS BUILDING IS CONDEMNED. PUBLIC ACCESS IS DENIED.

Blade strolled casually down the concrete steps to the sidewalk and took a left. He glanced at Geronimo, who was right behind him, then at the partially open door to the condemned building. "Where's Nathan?" he asked, and halted.

Geronimo stopped and turned. "Hickok?"

"He was with us a minute ago," Blade mentioned.

They waited expectantly for the gunman to emerge.

"Do you think he got lost?" Geronimo queried after a minute.

"If he took a wrong passage, all he had to do was give a yell," Blade said.

"What else could have happened?"

"Beats me," Blade responded.

"Maybe he walked into a wall and knocked himself out," Geronimo suggested.

"Be serious."

"I guess I should have held his hand," Geronimo said.

Blade sighed and started up the steps. "Stay put. I'll go find him."

"Hold it right there, Private!" commanded a stern voice.

The Warriors pivoted to the west.

A tall Soviet officer stood eight feet away, his hands at his sides, his countenance haughty, his green eyes regarding them critically. A holstered pistol rode on his right hip. "What are you men doing?" he demanded.

"Conducting a search of these buildings, sir," Blade replied, holding the Commando next to his right leg and hoping the officer would not notice the firearm's unique contours.

"What unit are you men with?"

"We're perimeter guards at the L.R.F.," Blade said, taking a gamble.

The officer twisted and stared at the commotion surrounding the damaged jeep. "They have every available soldier out here," he said, his right arm obscured by his body. There was a sudden motion and he whirled with the pistol clutched in his right hand. "But the two of you are not perimeter guards. You will lower your weapons to the ground now!"

Blade placed the Commando on the concrete. Out of the corner of his left eye he saw Geronimo also complying.

"You will be so good as to raise your arms," the officer directed.

Frowning, Blade obeyed. Several of the spectators had witnessed the officer pulling his gun and were staring at the Warriors. None of the other Russian soldiers were aware of the situation yet, but that would change any moment. The distance was too great for Blade to try and employ his Bowies; the officer would shoot him before he could grab either knife. He knew Geronimo was in the same boat with respect to the Arminius and the tomahawk. They needed a break, a distraction, or for the officer to make a mistake.

The Russian unwittingly obliged.

"Come here," the officer said. "Slowly."

Blade walked down the steps, his hands next to his shoulders, and deliberately stepped in front of Geronimo, obstructing the officer's view.

"Don't!" the Russian snapped, wagging the pistol. "Stand aside!"

Blade stared blankly at the officer.

"Move, damn you!" the Russian barked.

"Sorry," Blade said politely, and flattened.

His shirttail hanging out, Geronimo had the Arminius extended and cocked, and he fired a single shot.

The slug caught the officer between the eyes and knocked him five feet to tumble onto his back. Screams and shouts erupted from the spectators, and all eyes suddenly focused on the Warriors and the figure on the ground.

Blade was up and bounding to the Commando.

"Do we go find Hickok?" Geronimo queried, hastily retrieving the SAR as he slid the Arminius under his shirt.

A half-dozen AK-47's thundered simultaneously before Blade could answer, and he was forced to drop to the sidewalk, hearing the repeated smacking and zinging of the heavy slugs as they struck the building. Their position was untenable. If a live round didn't get them, a ricochet just might. "On me!" he cried, and dashed between a pair of green trucks.

"Don't shoot!" someone was shouting. "Don't shoot! You'll hit civilians!"

Blade turned to the east, jogging down the center line with a row of vehicles on both sides, heading toward the heart of the city. Although many of the drivers and passengers had vacated their vehicles to catch a glimpse of the bustling troops, there were still dozens patiently waiting in their cars or trucks for the military to allow them to drive on. A man in a blue car saw Blade coming and poked his head out the driver's window.

"Hey, buddy. What's happening?"

"Some big guy is shooting people," Blade replied as he came abreast of the car, and grinned wickedly.

"No shit?" the man said, then did a double take and frantically rolled up his window.

Blade sprinted past the blue car. The mission was rapidly dissolving into a first-rate farce. The element of surprise was totally lost, the odds of completing the assignment were less than nil, and to compound their predicament, Hickok was missing. He looked to the east, amazed at the size of the traffic jam caused by a mere fender-bender, and increased his speed.

"They're twenty yards behind us," Geronimo stated.

"Let's hope we can outrun them," Blade said over his left shoulder. He passed the last of the vehicles occupying the right lane.

"I don't like leaving Nathan."

"Can't be helped. We'll go back for him later."

"Provided we're alive."

"Cheer up," Blade quipped, breathing heavily as his boots pounded on the pavement. "What else could possibly go wrong?"

A pair of helicopters abruptly streaked in low over the L.R.F. installation, angling above Delhi Road. Each chopper was outfitted with a spotlight mounted on the nose, and they banked to direct the bright beams at the road.

"I had to open my big mouth," Blade said, slowing so as not to attract the attention of the pilots.

"Maybe they have no idea where we're at," Geronimo remarked.

The helicopters unexpectedly fixed their spotlights on the Warriors, bathing them in a brilliant glow.

Blade stopped and held his left arm in front of his eyes to reduce the glare.

"I never did like being the center of attention," Geronimo said, and sighted the SAR. He fired a half-dozen rounds and one of the spotlights went out. The choppers swerved and danced in the sky.

Shadowy forms were bearing down on the Warriors from the rear.

"Drop your weapons!" a raspy voice commanded.

In response, Blade spun and squeezed the trigger, the Commando booming and bucking.

Someone screeched.

The pursuing Russian soldiers dove for cover.

Blade nudged Geronimo's right shoulder and took off, racing to the east, a feeling of impending doom gnawing at his consciousness. Sooner or later the Soviets would hem them in. He needed a bright idea, and he needed it right away. To the left were idling vehicles and a block or two of condemned buildings. To the right was the L.R.F. facility. Scores of soldiers were to the rear. The persistent helicopters hovered just out of effective gun range. One of the choppers still had a spotlight trained on them. Frustration and a sense of helplessness welled within him.

"Surrender!" bellowed the raspy, metallic voice.

The speaker must be using a bullhorn, Blade deduced, and ran at his top speed, his flinty gray eyes narrowing when he spied a stand of trees far ahead and to the left. What better spot to make their last stand? The trees would allow them mobility while sheltering them from the enemy. He thought of Jenny and Gabe, and sorrow racked his heart as he realized he might never see them again.

An elderly couple appeared ahead, standing near their dark brown sedan, both of them well dressed. They were gazing to the west, obviously wondering about the cause of the delay and the uproar. The man spotted the Warriors first and recoiled against his car, his arms around his wife.

"Look out, dear!" he cried.

Blade swung around them. "We won't harm you," he said.

"Nice night for stargazing," Geronimo added courteously.

The elderly couple gaped at the Warriors, and when the giant and the Indian were five yards past them they looked to the west at the advancing Russian soldiers.

"Here!" the man yelled.

"The ones you want are here!" the woman elaborated.

Geronimo glanced back at them and chuckled. "They certainly know how to make a stranger feel welcome."

"I have an idea," Blade commented.

"I'm open to any suggestions," Geronimo said, straining to match his friend's speed.

"We should separate," Blade stated, inhaling loudly.

"Forget it."

"We'd have a better chance of one of us coming out of this alive," Blade noted.

"No way."

"This is an order."

"I can't hear you," Geronimo responded, huffing and puffing.

"I never pegged you as a dummy."

"That's Hickok's department."

Blade went to argue, then reconsidered. Geronimo knew the stakes, and Warriors were trained to always be loyal to one another. A Warrior never deserted another Warrior. The Elders instilled a profound appreciation for supreme values in every man and woman who served as a defender of the Home and a guardian of the Family. In the 105-year history of the Warrior order, only one had ever gone astray.

"Why aren't they shooting?" Geronimo asked.

Blade's thigh muscles were beginning to hurt. "My guess is they want us alive."

"Lucky us."

"I just hope they're so busy concentrating on us that they overlook Hickok."

"He probably stopped to take a leak and couldn't find the zipper in the dark."

They sped onward, cutting the distance to the trees in half, attended by the choppers and chased by scores of soldiers.

"We've got to reach those trees," Blade said.

"Don't tell me you need to take a leak too?"

"Are you still considering quitting the Warriors?"

"I can't imagine why."

Another 25 yards were covered, and then the growl of a jeep motor arose to their rear.

Blade glanced back.

Two jeeps were after them, both straddling the sidewalk on the south side of Delhi road.

"May I?" Geronimo inquired.

"Be my guest."

Geronimo halted and whirled, lowering himself to his right knee and aiming the SAR. "I wonder if their windshields are bulletproof?" he queried, and sent a burst into the foremost jeep.

The windshield shattered and the jeep veered sharply to the right, bouncing up and over the curb and barreling for the L.R.F. wall. A man in a uniform tumbled from the driver's seat mere seconds before impact. The crash was tremendous. A fireball enveloped the vehicle and billowed skyward.

"One down," Geronimo said, and pointed the SAR at the second jeep.

"If you pull that trigger, you're dead men!"

Blade spun toward the speaker, to the east, astounded to behold 11 Soviet soldiers blocking the route to the trees. Ten of the troopers were ready to fire, their AK-47's leveled. The eleventh stood in the middle of the road, his hands clasped behind his narrow back, his angular features inscrutable. "Put down your weapons this instant," he ordered calmly.

"What do we do?" Geronimo whispered.

"I will repeat myself only this once," the Soviet officer informed them. "Lower your weapons or my men will kill you where you stand."

Blade frowned and deposited the Commando at his feet.

Reluctantly, Geronimo did the same with the SAR.

The officer stalked forward. His hair was black, his eyes blue. Four rows of ribbons decorated his chest, aligned neatly above his left shirt pocket. A red star adorned each slim shoulder. "I'm pleased to see that you are reasonable men," he said. "I'm a reasonable man myself. My name is Ari Stoljarov. General Stoljarov. Some of our more imaginative citizens like to refer to me as the Butcher."

Chapter Thirteen

What was the blasted critter doing?

Taking a snooze?

Hickok stood as immobile as a statue, scarcely daring to breathe, feeling the weight of the creature on the top of his head, his neck muscles twitching.

How long had he stood there?

A minute?

Two?

He was tempted to give a yell, to let his pards know he was in trouble, but the slightest motion might agitate the thing perched on his noggin, might provoke it to bite him. Being bitten wasn't a big deal. Being bitten by a potentially poisonous spiker was. And Hickok believed the critter was a spider.

A mutant spider.

From the pressure on his hair, he knew that eight appendages were gripping the sides of his head, and spiders sported eight legs. Plus there was the matter of the cobwebs all over the place. By his reckoning, a spider was the only candidate. From the size of the thing, it must be a mutant. But if so, where did the midget monster come from? Cincinnati had not sustained a nuclear hit during the Big Blast, so the radiation levels shouldn't have climbed very high, definitely not high enough to permanently pollute the environment. Genetic deviations, as Plato liked to call the varmints, were usually the result of radiation or some other toxin disrupting the inheritance factors in the genes. If radiation didn't produce the creature on his head, what the dickens did? As far as he knew, no chemical weapons were used in the vicinity of Cincinnati.

Wait a minute.

He was forgetting something.

The fallout.

Think, you dunderhead! he chided himself. What did he know about fallout? What had the Elders taught him? Whenever a nuclear doohickey detonated at ground level, the explosion sucked all kinds of dust and debris up into the atmosphere. The winds would then scatter the radioactive particles all over the landscape. The important distinction to make was between a ground blast and an air burst. Air bursts hardly produced any fallout, and the Soviets had wisely employed primarily air bursts during World War Three. Exclusively blanketing America with ground-level strikes would have been a drastic case of overkill and defeated the Soviet Union's purpose. The Russians wanted to *conquer* America, not reduce it to a smoldering cinder.

Hickok felt the spider shift its weight.

If he recollected correctly, the Russians had generally reserved ground strikes for military targets, and there had been any number of primary military targets to the west of Ohio. There had also been two prime military sites north of Cincinnati.

But what were they?

Think!

He remembered a course taught by one of the Elders concerning the known Hot Spots in the country, those areas where there had been ground blasts. They also covered known and suspected air-burst targets. Columbus, Ohio, was one of the cities believed devastated by an air burst because of the proximity of Rickenbacker Air Force Base. Oddly, Dayton, Ohio, near which Wright Patterson Air force Base was located, was not hit. So the closest confirmed target to Cincinnati, namely Columbus, sustained an air burst, and the prevailing high-altitude winds would have carried the minimal amount of radioactive particles to the east, not to the southwest toward Cincinnati.

Which brought him back to square one.

What accounted for the danged spider?

Hickok was becoming impatient. He didn't want Blade and Geronimo to get too far ahead. Surely they had noticed his absence by now! He expected them to show up at any moment.

Gunfire suddenly punctuated the blackness, arising from the direction of Delhi Road.

Blade and Geronimo were in trouble!

Hickok hesitated for less than a second. He couldn't stand idly by and do nothing while his friends were fighting for their lives. He might be bitten if he so much as moved a muscle, but that was the risk he would have to take. His hands were at his sides, and he tensed his fingers and his shoulder muscles in preparation for making his play.

There was a slim hope.

If he could smash the spider before the arachnid bit him, he'd be home free. Everyone claimed he was one of the fastest men with a shooting iron who ever lived. Here was his chance to prove his speed with his hands.

Then again, the creature might not even be a spider and might not be posionous, in which case he was standing there like an idiot running in mental circles and worrying over nothing. He gritted his teeth, clenched his fists, and went into action.

Hickok whipped his fists up and around, his arms arcing at the thing with all the swiftness of a striking rattlesnake, yet as quick as he was, he wasn't quick enough. His fists were

midway to his head when he felt an intense stinging sensation
an inch or so above his hairline. The mutant started to rise,
using its legs to push itself erect. Hickok brought his fists down
with all the force in his sinews, smashing whatever-it-was to
a pulp, plastering his hair with its flattened, gory form. His
loathing compelled him to pound the creature again and again,
until he was certain it was dead, until his head ached. He
relaxed and leaned against the right-hand wall, expelling a long
breath.

He'd done it!

But the critter had nailed him.

He straightened and took a stride forward. A liquid substance
trickled past his ears and onto his neck. Feeling nauseous, he
hurried, eager to catch up to Blade and Geronimo. The stinging
on his scalp was spreading rapidly and growing worse.

Blast!

Hickok reached up and used his fingers as scoops, wiping
his hands back and forth, trying to remove the mashed, pasty
residue from his blond hair. His hands became sticky, and he
detected the scent of a putrid odor.

The shooting outside seemed to have ceased.

He abruptly felt extremely hot, as if his body temperature
had elevated five degrees, and his head was now burning
terribly. His eyes were having difficulty focusing.

Was that a ribbon of light up ahead?

Blade had mentioned seeing a light.

The thought of Blade and Geronimo pushed him onward.
The dummies needed him. He couldn't fail them now when
the chips were down.

Ooooh, his aching noggin!

Hickok noticed a strange tingling in his limbs, and his
movements were becoming sluggish. He shook his head,
striving to concentrate on reaching the light, but his body was
refusing to cooperate. A peculiar lethargy engulfed him and
he halted, weaving, flushed and disoriented.

What a pitiful way to buy the farm.

Bumped off by a measely spider.

The gunman mustered his flagging strength and tottered toward the light, and for a few seconds he believed he would make it. Then his knees buckled and he sagged to the dusty floor, doubling over, his whole body on fire, and his consciousness plunged into the flames of oblivion.

Chapter Fourteen

"You are impressed, are you not?"

"I'm impressed," Blade grudgingly admitted.

General Ari Stoljarov smirked. "We depleted our Treasury to construct this facility, a small price to pay for the capability to conquer the world."

"What loony bin did they find you in?" Geronimo quipped.

The Butcher halted and glared at Geronimo. "Have a care, Warrior. I could have your life snuffed out like that." He snapped his fingers.

"I'm shaking in my boots," Geronimo responded, and his eyes suddenly widened. "You know who we are?"

"Of course, simpleton," General Stoljarov said contemptuously.

Blade's lips compressed as he stared at the towering edifices around him. They were 30 yards inside the massive front gate, walking along a wide avenue amply lit by intermittent streetlights. The ten troopers comprising the general's personal guard ringed them with AK-47's at the ready. Geronimo and he had been frisked and their weapons confiscated by one of the soldiers. Although they were not bound, they were powerless to resist.

"It would take more than a Soviet uniform to disguise the likes of you, Blade, or you, Geronimo," General Stoljarov went on. "Our file on the two of you is quite extensive. After all, your accursed Family has been a thorn in our side for years. You have thwarted our plans repeatedly."

"We've tried," Blade said with a smile.

"Enjoy your arrogance while you can," General Stoljarov said. "I will take great delight in teaching both of you the meaning of humility."

"We've been threatened by experts," Blade replied, intentionally sounding bored. "You're just one more power-monger in our eyes."

"Power-monger?"

"The term the Elders apply to anyone who craves power, anyone who tries to impose their will on others, anyone who thinks everyone else should live by their dictates."

General Stoljarov made a snorting noise. "Your definition could apply to every living person."

"Not everyone has the potential inside them to become a power-monger," Blade said. "Only those who presume to recast the world in their own biased image."

The general's brown eyes locked on the giant. "For once the stories weren't exaggerated."

"General?"

General Stoljarov motioned for them to proceed. "As I indicated, I have read your dossier. I have also attended Defense Ministry meetings devoted to discussions of the most expedient methods of liquidating the Warriors and exterminating the Family, preferably both in one fell swoop." He paused. "I believe you're familiar with the name Malenkov?"

"General Malenkov," Blade said. "He captured Hickok once, sent a special squad to the Home to kidnap a Family member, and had a spy infiltrate the Freedom Federation. I've never had the displeasure of meeting the man personally, but yes, I'm familiar with General Malenkov.''

"Comrade Malenkov and I are close friends," General Stoljarov disclosed.

"Figures," Geronimo stated. "Snakes in the grass tend to breed together.''

The Butcher glared at Geronimo for a moment. "I mentioned General Malenkov because he will be very glad to see the two of you.''

"He's here?'' Blade asked.

"No. But I intend to contact him shortly and advise him of your apprehension. I am positive he will drop everything and fly here immediately.''

"Is Malenkov your superior officer?'' Blade inquired.

"Comrade Malenkov is a man of prominence in the North American Central Committee, and he is largely responsible for administering our occupational forces. He is a three-star general. I, unfortunately, have but one star.''

"So you plan to get some brownie points by informing General Malenkov that you lucked out and caught us,'' Geronimo said, baiting the Butcher. "Taking us prisoner will look real good on your service record, and might help you get your second star. Not that you'd deserve it.''

"Luck was not a factor in your capture!'' General Stoljarov snapped. "Have you forgotten your run-in with two of our helicopters? Every Soviet unit in Illinois, Indiana, Ohio, Pennsylvania, and New York was placed on alert after your unique vehicle was discovered so close to our lines.''

"You didn't have to go to so much trouble over us,'' Geronimo said. "But we appreciate the thought.''

Stoljarov ignored him. "When one of our routine patrols failed to report in from Dunlap this afternoon as scheduled, every soldier in the city was instructed to be on the watch for men answering your descriptions.'' He laughed. "Of course, I did not expect you to blunder into our arms so easily. How convenient of you to expose yourselves outside the front gate to the Laser Research Facility.''

"Is that what this dump is called?" Geronimo queried.

With surprising celerity and savagery, the Butcher stepped close to Geronimo and backhanded the Warrior across the mouth.

Geronimo's head lashed to the right and he stumbled and nearly went down. He caught himself and straightened, blood trickling from the corner of his mouth. "Is that the best you can do?" he asked.

"I can do much better, I assure you. Much, much better," General Stoljarov said.

Blade moved between Geronimo and the general. "You're a brave man when you're backed up by ten AK-47's. How are you at one-on-one?"

Stoljarov sneered. "I hope Comrade Malenkov will permit me to demonstrate my prowess."

"Don't use him as an excuse," Blade said. "I'm ready whenever you are."

General Stoljarov draped his hands behind his back, his eyes riveted on the giant's, betraying no trace of fear. "At the proper time, Warrior, you will get your wish." He wheeled and walked onward.

Blade looked at Geronimo as they followed. "Are you all right?"

Geronimo rubbed his chin and nodded. "Fine. But be careful," he replied softly. "That sucker is strong."

"So am I."

General Stoljarov slowed, waiting for them to reach his left side. "I trust there will not be any further slurs directed at my facility?"

"*Your* facility?" Blade repeated.

"I am the commander in charge of the Laser Research Facility." General Stoljarov divulged. He gestured proudly with his right arm. "All that you see is under my jurisdiction. I am in charge of the citadel destined to alter the course of human history. The most magnificent weapon ever conceived is at my disposal."

"I don't suppose you'd care to tell me about it?"

Stoljarov grinned. "At the proper time, Warrior," he reiterated, and stared fondly at the silver spire.

"What purpose does the spire serve?"

"You are looking at the ultimate achievement in technology," General Stoljarov boasted. "Our scientists have created the perfect instrument of destruction."

"The only perfect weapon is a disciplined master of the fighting arts," Blade declared.

"Spare me your puerile philosophy," Stoljarov stated. "Can a master of the fighting arts stand in Cincinnati and shoot down a jet in, say, Denver?" His eyes sparkled as he spoke.

Blade scrutinized the ominous silver spire, focusing on the immense opague crystal globe. "Then you are responsible for destroying the 757," he said, awed by the implications. Oddly enough, despite the fact he'd suspected the Soviets were to blame ever since the meeting with President Toland, and although Fedorov had all but confirmed his suspicions, the verification by General Stoljarov staggered his emotions. Never in a million years would he have believed the Soviets capable of such a feat.

"Among other things," Stoljarov commented enigmatically.

They were passing between two similar buildings, square monoliths rearing 20 stories above the ground.

"Seems to me that your L.R.F. is a big waste of time and expense," Geronimo remarked.

"You think so?" Stoljarov responded.

"I know so. You managed to shoot down the Federation's 757. Big deal. The destruction of one jet doesn't justify the cost of this project," Geronimo said with a tinge of sarcasm.

"Do you take us for fools, Warrior? Our purpose in constructing this facility was not for the sole purpose of shooting down aircraft. We have far grander designs for the L.R.F."

"Like what?" Geronimo prompted.

"Like bringing the Freedom Federation to its knees. Like reducing your Home to a pile of rubble. Like achieving the final triumph of Communism and the establishment of Russian domination world wide.''

"All that with your dinky red light?''

"Soon our dinky red light, as you facetiously call it, will be the terror of the planet.''

"A friend of ours has an expression he uses every now and then,'' Geronimo said. "It applies to you Russians.''

"Which is?''

"You're getting too big for your britches.''

General Stoljarov smiled scornfully. "How quaint.''

"Your insane scheme will fail,'' Blade mentioned. "You know that, don't you?''

"I know nothing of the sort,'' Stoljarov answered.

"The Freedom Federation will do whatever it takes to stop you.''

"How? By sending more Warriors? Don't make me laugh,'' General Stoljarov said, and looked at the giant. "And speaking of Warriors, where is your companion?''

"Our companion?'' Blade responded.

"Don't play the innocent with me. There were four men in the jeep involved in the fender bender. The driver was slain. And there are a dozen witnesses who claim that three men fought with our guards and were seen running from the scene. I know the Warriors are divided into groupings called Triads, and our intelligence data lists the members of one such Triad, Alpha Triad, as yourself, Geronimo, and the pistoleer, the genius Hickok. Where is Hickok?''

Blade and Geronimo exchanged glances.

"Was that a joke?'' Geronimo asked.

"What?'' General Stoljarov replied.

"That crack about Hickok being a genius,'' Geronimo clarified. "You were kidding us, right?''

"General Malenkov himself told me that Hickok is not to be taken lightly,'' Stoljarov said. "Hickok is extremely devious and clever. He outwitted our forces in Washington, D.C., and commandeered a helicopter. General Malenkov had Hickok in the palm of his hand, yet Hickok slipped through."

"Yeah, but—" Geronimo began.

"General Malenkov says Hickok is all the more dangerous because of the act he puts on. He pretends to be a buffoon, to be dense and dumb, when all the time his mind is razor sharp. He fooled Comrade Malenkov once, but he will not trick us again."

"Amazing," was all Geronimo could think of to say.

"Where is he?" Stoljarov stated impatiently.

"I don't know anyone by that name," Geronimo said.

The Butcher exhaled noisily. "Very well. Indulge in your games for a few minutes longer. I don't require your information anyway. My men are scouring Delhi Road for the pistoleer, and they will find him eventually."

They walked in silence for a minute.

"Where are you taking us?" Blade inquired.

"You've expressed such an interest in Lenin's Needle, I thought I would conduct a guided tour."

"Why do you call it Lenin's Needle?"

"As a tribute to one of the greatest heroes of the Communist movement, the man who founded the Communist Party in Russia. He set the pattern for all future Communists to follow," General Stoljarov said proudly.

"Some pattern," Blade remarked. "We studied the history of Russia in the Family school, as part of our understanding of the factors leading to the confrontation between the superpowers. Lenin set up a secret police force and killed everyone who disagreed with his views. He was just another power-monger, plain and simple."

"I would not expect you to comprehend Lenin's contribution to humanity," General Stoljarov stated.

"I understand it, all right. Lenin's contribution consisted of a totalitarian government determined to subjugate every other country. Lenin's warped political philosophy indirectly led to World War Three."

General Stoljarov stopped in his tracks and shook his head in astonishment. "Now I've heard everything! To blame

Comrade Lenin for World War Three is ridiculous. To be fair, you should also blame General George Washington." He resumed walking.

"Washington didn't leave as his legacy a government devoted to the suppression of individual liberty."

"It is obvious we will never see eye to eye on political matters," Stoljarov said.

"Or anything else," Blade added.

They drew nearer to Lenin's Needle, following the avenue as it looped around a row of deciduous trees.

"I have a surprise for you," General Stoljarov mentioned.

"Can we pass?" Geronimo asked. "Any surprise of yours is bound to be hazardous to our health."

"You misjudge me, Geronimo," the general said.

"Then what's this big surprise of yours?" Geronimo queried skeptically.

The Butcher smirked at both of them. "Would you believe a firing squad?"

Chapter Fifteen

Somewhere, someone was talking to him. He could hear their voice, but the words were muffled and slurred, as if they were trying to speak with a mouth full of marbles.

Why was it so blamed hot?

He became aware of a weight on his chest, and suddenly the memories returned in a rush: Cincinnati, the Russians, the vacant building, the spider, and being bitten! Another spider must be about to bite him! His eyes shot open and he grabbed at the form before him, his vision momentarily blurry.

"Mister! It's okay!"

Hickok shook his head vigorously, clearing his mind and his eyesight simultaneously. He was on his back on the hall floor, his right hand gripping the left wrist of an elderly man attired in ragged clothing. The man held a flickering lighter aloft in his right hand, and his right knee rested on Hickok's chest.

"Please, mister! I mean you no harm!" the elderly man blurted. "Don't hurt me!"

"Who are you?" Hickok demanded.

"Elmer. Elmer Howard," the man said. His black pants were ripped at the knees and covered with dirt. A brown shirt with three buttons missing and crude patches on both elbows covered his frail torso.

"What were you doing?"

"I found you out cold and I was trying to revive you."

"How do I know you weren't tryin' to finish me off?" Hickok asked.

"I'm no killer, mister."

Hickok studied the oldster's face, noting the dozens of wrinkles, the honest green eyes, and the matted gray hair. "No, I reckon you're not, Elmer. My name is Hickok."

"I saw you fighting the Commies," Elmer commented. "You and your buddies."

"My pards!" Hickok exclaimed, and shoved to his feet. The hallway abruptly spun and tilted, and he clutched at the wall for support.

"You'd best take it easy, Hickok," Elmer advised. "The bite of a Brown is nothing to mess with."

"A Brown?"

"That's what we call the kind of spider that bit you."

"How'd you know I was bitten by a spider?" Hickok queried.

Elmer nodded at Hickok's head. "You have bits and pieces of spider plastered to your hair."

"I'm surprised I'm still breathin'," Hickok remarked.

"Oh, the Browns don't kill you, but they can make you feel like puke for a while," Elmer said.

"Where do they come from?" Hickok inquired, feeling groggy.

"Folks claim they've been around since after the damn war," Elmer answered.

"Why are they called Browns?"

"Because that's the color they are," Elmer explained, his tone implying the answer should have been readily apparent.

"I've got to find my friends," Hickok said, rubbing his

burning forehead. "Where's the door?"

"Down there," Elmer said, nodding at the end of the hall where a closed door was barely discernible in the faint illumination supplied by the lighter. "But if I was you, I wouldn't go out that way."

"Why not?"

"For one thing, that door opens onto Delhi Road, and there are Commies all over the place. You wouldn't get very far in the shape you're in," Elmer responded. "For another thing, you'd be wasting your time looking for your friends."

"Why?"

"The Commies caught them."

Hickok straightened and swung toward the door, unslinging the AR-15. "When? How?"

"A while ago," Elmer said. "Your friends didn't stand a prayer."

"Tell me everything, from the beginning."

Elmer scratched his stubbly chin. "Well, let's see. I was on the second floor of the condemned store three doors down when I heard a crash—"

"What were you doing there?" Hickok asked, interrupting.

"Getting set to settle in for the night. I sleep in these buildings when I'm in the neighborhood. Some of the other bums crash out in these buildings too. The Commies don't bother us much. But I know they're getting set to raze all these empty buildings just so we won't hang around here anymore."

"Finish your story."

"My story? Oh, yeah. There I was, about to bed down, when there was this racket outside and I peeked out the window and saw there'd been an accident. The next thing I know, everybody is shooting and hollering and running like crazy, and you and your two buddies ran into the alley and a whole bunch of Commies went after you." Elmer paused to take a breath. "I was sort of curious, so I snuck outside and mingled with the crowd, and I saw a few of the bodies. Not much happened for a while, and then I noticed your two buddies coming out of this building. A Commie tried to take them, but they nailed the son of a bitch but proper and lit out." He paused again and sighed. "They wasted a heap of Commies, but the head honcho himself caught them."

"Who?"

"Mr. High-and-Mighty General Ari Stoljarov. Everyone calls him the Butcher. I've seen him a few times before going in and out of the base across the street, and I saw his picture in the paper. He's a mean one."

"You read the paper?" Hickok asked.

Elmer scrunched up his nose. "What, a bum can't be literate? I find papers in trash cans all the time. And yeah, I can read real good, thank you."

"I didn't mean to offend you," Hickok said. "What happened to my pards after General What's-His-Name captured them?"

"General Stoljarov. They were taken into the base. The last I saw, they were still alive. But from what I've heard about the damn Butcher, they won't be for long."

"I've got to find them," Hickok declared, and took a stride toward the door.

"You're being a jerk," Elmer stated.

Hickok turned. "You think so?"

"I know so. What are you planning to do? March over to the gate and ask the Commies to surrender?"

"There's an idea," Hickok said, and grinned.

"I can help you get into the base."

"Why are you putting your life in danger for me?"

Elmer gazed at the lighter. "Because I hate the Commies. The bastards took my wife from me thirty years ago to use for their breeding program. They made her carry their rotten seed, and after the baby was born they took the child and tossed her out the door. She was the kindest person you'd ever want to meet, and they tore her soul to pieces. After they were done with her, she was never the same. She lost the will to live and died six years later."

"I'm sorry," Hickok said softly.

"Without her, my life wasn't worth a damn. I've been

bumming ever since. And whenever I get the chance to put the screws to the Commies, I do. I lost track of how many tires I've flattened by letting the air out. If I find a Commie vehicle left by itself, I like to pour dirt down the carburetor,'' Elmer disclosed, and tittered. ''I knew you guys weren't Commies the minute I saw you, even though you're wearing Commie uniforms. And when I saw your buddies come out of this building without you, I got curious about what happened to you. I snuck in when I figured nobody was looking, shut the door, and pulled out my lighter. You're lucky I found you before the Commies. They're still searching this block. A squad will likely come in here at any second.''

''Do you know this area well?''

''Like the back of my hand,'' Elmer said. ''I know every nook and cranny in these abandoned buildings, every manhole and sewer·tunnel for miles around.''

''Then we'd best skedaddle,'' Hickok stated.

''Ske-what?''

''Vamose.''

''Va-who?''

''We'd best get the blazes out of here.''

''Why didn't you say so in the first place?'' Elmer asked, and started to turn, flicking off the lighter. ''Follow me.''

With a resounding crash the front door was forcefully kicked open, slamming against the wall, and framed in the doorway stood a strapping Russian soldier with an AK-47. ''You there!'' he bellowed, stepping forward, striving to see them clearly. ''What are you doing?''

''Twiddlin' our thumbs,'' Hickok responded, and fired from the hip.

The impact hurled the Russian backwards, his arms flung wide, the AK-47 clattering to the floor. He hurtled through the doorway and dropped from sight, and was promptly replaced by a second trooper materializing at the door.

''Go!'' Hickok goaded Elmer, and squeezed off four rounds. The second soldier fell.

''Stay close to me,'' Elmer advised, hastening down the hall to the junction.

"Just go!" Hickok prompted, his eyes on the doorway, firing as yet another Russian appeared.

Elmer took a left at the junction.

Backpedaling rapidly, Hickok saw several dark forms dart into the hall. He was almost to the junction, and he cut loose, swiveling the barrel from right to left.

A trooper screamed, and then the Russians were returning the Warrior's fire, their AK-47's thundering, bright flashes of orange marking their muzzles.

Hickok ducked around the corner and heard dozens of rounds thud into the wall. He stuck the AR-15 out, intending to send a parting burst at the Soviets, but an AK-47 chattered and the AR-15 was torn from his hands and cast against the wall.

Blast!

Hickok whirled and raced along the hall, unbuttoning his shirt as he ran, wondering how far ahead Elmer was, knowing the Russians would catch them easily. Elmer obviously did not have the stamina for a sustained chase. His hands closed on the Pythons' pearl grips and he smiled.

Let the Commies come!

He slid the Colts out. They weren't going to nail him without a fight. His pockets were crammed with ammunition, enough to account for a couple of dozen troopers. He glanced over his right shoulder, attempting to distinguish shapes in the gloom.

A hand shot out of the darkness, seized the gunman by the left arm, and hauled him from the corridor.

"What—!" Hickok exclaimed.

"Quiet, you idiot!" Elmer hissed. "It's just me."

"Where are we?" Hickok whispered. Wherever they were, the darkness was absolute, engendering an unpleasant sensation of claustrophobia.

"I think it was a closet once. Now hush," Elmer said.

There was a muted click as a door was closed.

"This way, comrades!" shouted a voice in the corridor.

Hickok tensed as heavy boots thumped past the closet. He waited with bated breath for their hiding place to be discovered. At least a minute elapsed, and all the while Russian soldiers streamed down the hallway. The tramping of the Soviet troopers gradually faded into the distance.

"Here we go," Elmer declared. "And try to keep up with me this time."

"It's hard to see you, let alone follow you," Hickok said.

"Crybaby."

Hickok felt fingers grasp his left forearm. "Is that you?"

"If it isn't, you're in serious dog shit. Keep quiet and I'll lead you out."

"How can you see?" Hickok queried. "There's no light."

"I'm used to this," Elmer said. "Most of my life is spent in the dark."

"Then lead the way," Hickok said. "But if we run into more Russians, drop flat and let me take care of them."

"They're all yours. Like I said, I'm not a killer," Elmer stated, and sighed. "Too bad. I owe these pricks plenty for what they did to Joyce."

Hickok heard another click and felt a slight gust of air touch his cheeks, and then the bum was leading him at a fast clip out of the closet and to the left. They took a second left at the next junction, and proceeded to wind through a series of inky passageways until they entered a large empty room on the south side of the building. Diffuse light from the streetlamps on Delhi Road revealed the filthy floor was littered with broken furniture and piles of trash.

Elmer released the gunman's arm and cocked his head to one side, listening. "I think we lost the bastards."

"This place reeks," Hickok commented.

"It isn't the Ritz, sonny," Elmer said. "I crash here often. Except for the rats, no one bothers me."

The rats?"

"Yeah. If you curl up into a ball when you sleep, they don't try and gnaw on your ears and nose."

"You're pullin' my leg, old-timer."

Elmer chuckled. "You're not too bright, are you?"

"Where do we go from here?" Hickok asked.

"I figured we'd shack up here for the night."

"No way," Hickok stated.

"Why not?" Elmer responded, grinning. "You afraid of the rats?"

"I'm afraid of what could happen to my pards if I don't get to them pronto," Hickok said. "You mentioned you can help me sneak into the L.R.F."

"That I can," Elmer confirmed. "But it will cost you."

"Cost me?" Hickok repeated in surprise. "What are you talkin' about? I thought you wanted to help me because you hate the Commies."

Elmer took two paces and crouched alongside a mound of debris. He began idly poking in the the mound, dislodging scraps of paper and the broken arm of a chair. "That's true," he agreed. "But I've been doing some thinking."

Hickok's eyes narrowed. He was suddenly suspicious of the bum. Elmer's attitude had changed drastically, and made him think that he had misplaced his trust in his erstwhile rescuer.

Apparently he had.

Because Elmer abruptly stood and turned, clutching a rusty knife in his right hand.

Chapter Sixteen

General Ari Stoljarov threw back his head and laughed. "If you could see your faces!" he told the Warriors.

The ten soldiers comprising the Butcher's personal guard joined in the mirth.

Blade looked at Geronimo, who frowned and shook his head.

"Do you truly believe I would have you executed by a firing squad?" General Stoljarov asked.

"Who knows?" Blade rejoined.

"I guarantee you that I will devise an inventive demise for the both of you," General Stoljarov said. "A firing squad would be too routine, too mundane."

"Not to mention messy," Geronimo observed.

General Stoljarov nodded at the row of trees. "My surprise is on the other side."

They bore to the left, skirting the trees. The avenue broadened, becoming an extensive parking lot situated at the base of the colossal spire. Dozens of cars and trucks filled parking spaces near the spire, but the center of the expanse of asphalt was occupied by a vehicle not normally found in a parking lot: a jet aircraft.

"The Hurricane!" Blade exclaimed, taking several strides forward. The missing VTOL appeared to be intact. A dozen troopers surrounded the craft, their AK-47's over their shoulders.

"Do you like the latest addition to the Soviet Air force?" General Stoljarov inquired.

Blade glanced at the officer. "The *Soviet* Air Force?"

"There is a saying common among American youth," General Stoljarov stated, and grinned. "Finders keepers. We shot the Hurricane down. Whether you like the idea or not, the VTOL is now ours."

Blade was relieved the Hurricane was in one piece. There were only two such aircraft at the Freedom Federation's disposal, and both were essential to maintaining the shuttle service between Federation members. The Free State of California had worked diligently to ensure the VTOLs were airworthy, and every Federation faction appreciated the critical importance of the pair of technological marvels.

The Hurricanes qualified as the last operational remnants of the prewar civilization's scientific genius. Although the Soviets possessed a fleet of helicopters, and although California and a few diverse groups or city-states could field functional planes or other craft, there were only the two VTOL's in existence. Twelve feet in height, 47 feet in length, with a wingspan of 32 feet, the Hurricanes could attain a speed of 600 miles an hour or hover stationary as if they were gigantic hummingbirds. Each VTOL packed a tremendous wallop, consisting of cannons, cluster bombs, rockets, and four Sidewinder missiles.

"Once our pilots have mastered this aircraft, it will become an invaluable weapon in our campaign to defeat the Freedom Federation," General Stoljarov bragged.

"We'll destroy it before we'll allow you to use it against us," Blade vowed.

"How? With the other Hurricane? Unfortunately, we will

have long since vaporized your Hurricane by the time ours begins conducting sorties.''

Blade craned his neck and stared up at the spire. The structure gave the illusion of reaching the starry firmament, an effect heightened by the crystal globe at the peak which was radiating a pale white glow. "With that?"

"What else?" General Stoljarov retorted.

"We have nothing to worry about," Geronimo said.

General Stoljarov swung toward him. "Why not?"

"Because if the pilots aren't any more intelligent than you are, they'll never figure out how to fly the Hurricane," Geronimo stated, and smiled.

The Butcher's expression hardened and he pointed at Lenin's Needle. "Proceed."

Blade and Geronimo complied, walking toward a brown door at the bottom of the silver tower.

"For your information, our pilots will master the VTOL easily thanks to the excellent instruction they are receiving," General Stoljarov said.

Blade gazed at the Hurricane. Their mission had acquired an extra dimension. Destroying the superweapon was just the first step; they must also retreive the Hurricane or wreck it. Under no circumstances would he let the VTOL remain in Soviet hands. The combination of the superweapon and the Hurricane would render the Soviets unbeatable.

But first things first.

He scrutinized the door ahead, calculating. The entrance to Lenin's Needle appeared wide enough to admit one person at a time, and promised to present a golden opportunity to make a bid for freedom. His gambit depended on the soldiers. Would one of the Russians enter first or would the troopers follow behind the Warriors? He looked at Geronimo and cleared his throat.

Geronimo glanced at his friend.

Blade winked, grinned, and gave a barely perceptible nod. He watched as Geronimo stared at the door, and Blade was pleased to note the comprehension flitting across his features.

"Frankly, I'm disappointed in the two of you," General Stoljarov mentioned. "I expected more of a fight out of you. Your reputation is greatly exaggerated."

"How did you earn your reputation as the Butcher?" Blade queried, hoping to distract the officer with conversation.

"Before I was assigned to head the Laser Research Facility, I was in charge of interrogations for this sector. When we needed answers, I obtained them. Regrettably, many of those who supplied the information we wanted did not survive the interrogation procedure."

"In other words, you tortured them to death," Blade said.

"Only the weaklings. Eventually, through word of mouth, the general populace came to regard me with disdain—"

"More like hatred," Geronimo said, correcting him.

"In any event, their petty concerns are of no consequence to me. I have a job to do and I do it. Professionally. Competently," General Stoljarov said.

"Don't forget ruthlessly," Geronimo added.

"I will relish interrogating you, Geronimo," the Butcher declared, "as I have few others in recent memory. I intend to give you the deluxe treatment."

Blade strolled calmly forward, passing row after row of parked vehicles. He estimated that 50 feet separated him from the door. "I have a question," he said.

"What is it?"

"Why wasn't Lenin's Needle constructed years ago? If this device is so powerful, why did you wait until now to build it?"

"For one reason, and one reason only. His name is Leonid Grineva."

"Who's he?"

"Our foremost scientist. He undoubtedly possesses the greatest mind since Albert Einstein. It was Leonid who achieved the breakthrough in cold-fusion-generated laser light. It was he who perfected the technique of controlled projection," General Stoljarov disclosed. "He completed the designs eighteen months ago."

"Your leaders must have a lot of confidence in this scientist," Blade casually commented.

Forty feet to go.

"Their confidence has been justified by his accomplishments," General Stoljarov said. "The Hurricane and the 757 are but the tip of the iceberg. For his next demonstration, Leonid plans to obliterate a land target."

Land target? Blade didn't like the sound of that.

"And if the demonstration is successful, as we fully expect it to be, we can commence our campaign to eradicate any and all opposition to the expansion of Soviet domination. Within a year this country will be ours. Within three years the planet," General Stoljarov asserted.

"Don't forget Mars and Venus," Geronimo said.

"Mock me while you can, but mark my words. We will not be denied our rightful destiny. Communism will ultimately prevail."

Thirty feet.

"Communism will never prevail," Blade stated. "Dictatorial regimes are their own worst enemies. When you sow hatred, you reap hatred, and the backlash of resentment will wash over you like a tidal wave."

"What nonsense. This world belongs to the strong, to those who reach out and take it. We are in power because we are the strongest, and we will remain in power because our strength will never fail."

"Dream on," said Blade.

"You won't be around to witness the final outcome anyway, Warrior," General Stoljarov commented.

"I wouldn't bet on it," Blade responded.

Twenty feet.

"One other thing I'm curious about," Blade mentioned. "What is the Hurricane doing here? I know the VTOL was en route from Denver to Miami when it was shot down, so there was no reason for it to be over Ohio airspace. Where was the Hurricane when you fired your new toy?''

"Near Louisville, Kentucky. The pilot was able to bring the Hurricane down in a field a mile from Louisville, and our people were on the scene within minutes. He was a fortunate man. We intended to vaporize the aircraft, but there were still a few kinks in the system then. The laser sheared off a portion of the tail and fuselage, yet the pilot landed safely. The Hurricane was brought here because the L.R.F. is the most secure installation we have. No one gets in or out without the proper credentials.''

Blade looked back at the Hurricane. "Who repaired the damage to the VTOL?''

"We did, obviously. We wanted the craft airworthy, and we're not lacking in technical skills. The tail and fuselage were repaired a month ago. We were able to salvage a few compatible parts from old MIGs, and the rest were especially manufactured.''

Ten feet.

"What, exactly, is a laser?" Blade inquired.

"Wouldn't you like to know?" General Stoljarov rejoined.

"Where is the pilot now?''

"None of your business.''

Blade was five feet from the door. If one of the troopers came around in front, his plan was doomed. He needed to be the first one to reach the door, so he increased his pace and gripped the doorknob with his right hand.

"Hold it,'' General Stoljarov snapped.

Smiling innocently, Blade turned, opening the door as he did, allowing Geronimo to stride inside.

"Stop right there!'' the Butcher barked, standing six feet off.

The nearest soldier started toward the giant, raising the barrel of his AK-47, "You heard the general!''

"So I did,'' Blade said, holding his left hand palm out. "And I wouldn't want to disobey the general, now would I?''

Geronimo had halted in the doorway.

"One of my men will take the lead,'' General Stoljarov said. "Let him pass.''

Blade gave a little bow. "Be my guest."

"Stand aside," the trooper directed, coming forward, the AK-47 trained on Geronimo.

It was now or never. Blade surreptitiously scanned the soldiers, noting that only three had a clear field of fire. The rest were behind or to the side of the general, and they would not dare risk firing for fear of hitting the Butcher. His abdominal muscles tightened as he girded his body, and when the unsuspecting trooper took another pace, Blade brought his left hand down and in, snatching the AK-47 by the barrel and tugging on the gun even as he swept his right fist into the Russian's stomach.

The soldier gurgled and bent in half.

Blade wrenched the AK-47 free, gripped the trooper by the shirt and tossed him into the general, then darted into the doorway as a short burst from another soldier smacked into the door. Geronimo was already racing down a well-lit corridor. Blade angled the AK-47 out the door and blasted a charging Russian, his round taking the man high in the chest and flipping the trooper to the ground.

General Stoljarov was on his back on the asphalt, struggling to extricate himself from under the guard Blade had slugged. "Get them!" he shouted. "I want them alive or your lives are forfeit!"

His men rushed the door.

Blade stood to the left of the door, his back to the wall, and grasped the AK-47 by the barrel. A Russian appeared in the doorway, and Blade swung the AK-47 with all of his prodigious might, the stock connecting with the trooper's face with a pronounced thud. The soldier fell on the spot, his visage a bloody ruin.

That should hold them for a few seconds!

Blade spun and raced along the hallway, his boots thumping on clean, white tiles. The walls were a pale red. Overhead fluorescent lamps provided the bright illumination. He passed a series of brown doors without encountering anyone else and came to a fork. A hasty glance in both directions confirmed two empty corridors.

But no Geronimo.

Which way had Geronimo taken? Blade hesitated, nervously chewing on his lower lip. Had Geronimo ducked through one of the doors he'd passed? He hoped not. A structure as immense as the silver spire would contain dozens upon dozens of passages and rooms, and if they became separated now they might stay separated.

''There he is!'' a soldier shouted to his rear.

Damn!

Blade took the right-hand corridor, hoping his choice was the correct one. The absence of Russian personnel bothered him. Why was this lowest level vacant? Had General Stoljarov purposely escorted them into Lenin's Needle by way of a seldom-used entrance? The corridor curved to the right, and he sped around the corner with the AK-47 clutched in his left hand, looking to find Geronimo.

Instead, not 12 feet away, startled by his abrupt arrival, stood a six-man Russian squad.

Chapter Seventeen

Hickok elevated the Pythons and trained them on the bum. "Don't even think it, old-timer," he warned.

Elmer gaped at the revolvers, then at the knife in his hand, and tittered.

"What's so blamed funny?"

"You figured I was going to try and cut you with this dinky knife?" Elmer asked.

"Looked that way," Hickok said.

"You must be nuts."

"Nope. Just real cautious," Hickok stated.

"Watch, sonny," Elmer said, turning and walking to the southwest corner of the room. He knelt and inspected the floorboards. "Now where is it?"

Hickok ambled over, the Colts leveled, unwilling to lower his guard, still distrustful. "What are you lookin' for?"

"Here it is!" Elmer declared, and leaned down to carefully insert the tip of the blunt knife into a crack in the floor. He grunted and strained, and a section of wood two feet square lifted from its recessed groves. Elmer took hold of the trapdoor and shoved it aside, exposing a pitch-black hole.

"What's that?" Hickok inquired.

"Haven't you ever seen a crawl space before?"

"Not that I recollect."

"Repairmen and such use crawl spaces for checking pipes and wiring and whatnot."

"We're going down there?"

"Sure enough."

"Must we?" Hickok questioned, lowering the Pythons.

Elmer glanced at the gunman and chuckled. "Don't worry, sonny. The Browns and the rats will leave you alone if you make a little noise. Do what I do."

"What's that?"

"I fart a lot."

Hickok slid the Colts under his shirt, insuring the barrels were securely wedged underneath his belt.

"I've been down this hole tons of times," Elmer informed him. "I've never had any problem. The roaches bug me, though."

"Roaches?"

"Cockroaches. The city is crawling with them, and I don't mind telling you that they give me the creeps."

"A few teensy bugs won't bother me."

"Teensy?" Elmer repeated, and laughed softly. "I'll show you how teensy they are." So saying, he extended his left arm into the hole, all the way to the shoulder, his forehead creasing as he felt here and there. "Usually there's a couple near the opening. These buggers climb all over you when you're in the crawl space, so don't pay them no mind. They don't bite." He muttered an unintelligible word and straightened, smiling. "Take a look." His left hand came out of the hole.

Hickok felt goose bumps erupt all over his skin, and his eyes widened at the sight of the four-inch insect, with its flat, brown, oval body, its long, swept-back antennae, overlapping wings, and six writhing legs.

"This is a medium-sized roach," Elmer said. "Some of

these suckers grow over six inches long.''

"And there are a passel of them down there?''

"A what?''

"A lot of those bugs?''

"Yep. But don't let them rattle you. They don't bite,'' Elmer told the gunman, then pressed the cockroach onto the floor and crushed the insect with the palm of his hand. "Want me to tell you a secret?''

Hickok stared at the mushy pieces of cockroach oozing between the bum's fingers. "What?''

Elmer looked up and grinned. "The roaches make great eating.''

"You *eat* them?''

"Don't knock it until you've tried it. When you're down on your luck and can't find a square anywhere, you take what you can get. A few of these will fill you right up,'' Elmer divulged. "You should eat one sometime and see for yourself.''

Hickok's stomach flip-flopped. "Not on your life.''

"Suit yourself, sonny,'' Elmer said, and shrugged. He wiped his hand off on the floor, then bent toward the crawl space. "Let's go.''

"Hold it.''

Elmer paused and gazed at the gunfighter. "Something wrong?''

"What was that business about your help costing me?''

"I want you to do me a favor. If you bump into General Stoljarov, I want you to kill him.''

"Any particular reason?''

"Do I need one? He didn't get the nickname the Butcher because he's a nice guy,'' Elmer said, and frowned. "A lot of decent folks have died at his hands, and several of them were friends of mine. The Butcher is the most hated Commie in Cincinnati, probably in all of Ohio.''

"How would I know him if I saw him?''

"That's easy. Just look for the crap seeping out his ears.''

Hickok grinned and nodded. "If I run into the vermin, I'll

plug him for you.''

''Thanks,'' Elmer said. He lowered his torso into the crawl space, dropping headfirst into the Stygian hole, disappearing slowly. ''Keep your head low,'' he advised, his voice muted.

Frowning, Hickok advanced to the crawl space and knelt for a better view, disconcerted by the fact that the darkness obscured everything, bothered by a nagging, lingering mistrust of the bug-eater. What if Elmer was setting him up? He'd be a sitting duck down there.

''Are you coming or what?'' Elmer called back.

''I'm comin','' Hickok said.

''Sometime this year would be nice,'' Elmer declared. ''If you want to save your buddies, that is.''

The reference to Blade and Geronimo galvanized Hickok into action, and he gingerly stretched his arms downward until his hands made contact with bare earth.

''Are you part turtle?'' Elmer queried, and snickered.

Hickok ignored the crack and eased lower until he was flat on his stomach. The air was musty, the dirt dank. ''Why is it moist down here?'' he whispered.

''Probably all that cockroach piss,'' Elmer replied, and sounded like he was gagging on his own laughter.

''A regular comedian,'' Hickok muttered, scanning in all directions, waiting for his eyes to adjust. A trickle of light seeping through cracks on the south side scarcely relieved the oppressive gloom, although he was able to discern that the crawl space extended under the entire building. ''Which way?''

''Follow me,'' Elmer replied softly. ''Just be careful you don't accidentally get your nose in any rat shit.'' He wheezed and snorted.

Hickok could perceive a vague shadow where Elmer must be, and he crawled toward the bum. The shadow moved, bearing to the east, and he stayed within half a yard of Elmer's shoes. A pungent odor crinkled his nostrils. ''Don't you ever wash your feet?''

Elmer sniggered. ''Excuse me for living. If I'd known

someone was going to get intimate with my tootsies, I would have taken my annual bath early.''

Something skittered across the gunman's left hand.

''What the dickens was that?'' Hickok blurted.

''What happened?''

''Something ran over my hand.''

''A cockroach, most likely.''

''I can't wait to get out of here.''

''Wimp.''

They continued to crawl across the clammy, acrid earth, attended by squeaks, vague rustlings, and scratching noises from every direction.

Hickok resisted an impulse to sneeze. He inadvertently stiffened when a thing that squealed ran over his legs. The crawl space gave him the willies! He preferred a straightforward, stand-up fight to all this skulking and slinking about in the dark. Having hordes of icky bugs clambering over his body was as appealing as dining on a cockroach.

A thin . . .something . . .with lots of legs unexpectedly climbed up his collar and onto his right cheek.

Reacting instinctively, Hickok slapped at the insect and crushed it. He used his fingers to flick the pulp away.

''What are you doing?'' Elmer asked.

''There was a blasted bug on my face.''

''Must of been in love.''

''Keep going,'' Hickok directed.

''Some people have no sense of humor,'' Elmer whispered.

For the gunman, the time seemed to drag on interminably. Scores of insects scaled his moving form, scrambling and scrabbling, seemingly oblivious to the fact that he was a human. Over a dozen climbed in his hair and were promptly dislodged.

Elmer began giggling.

''What's so funny?'' Hickok demanded.

''I've got a cockroach down my shirt, and the bugger tickles.''

''Too bad it isn't a black widow.''

"Boy, a little dirt and a few bugs and you go all to pieces."

"You're enjoying this, aren't you?"

"Damn straight."

"Are you part Blackfoot by any chance?"

"What's a Blackfoot?"

"Never mind."

A minute later Elmer stopped. "Hot damn!"

"What?"

"We're here."

"You'd better not be joshin' me."

"Wouldn't think of it, sonny."

Hickok perceived the outline of a wall in front of them, and he heard a slight grating noise. A square of welcome light materialized, and a draft of fresh air tingled his skin.

"Stay low," Elmer cautioned, and squeezed through the opening.

Hickok wasted no time in following, and found himself in a confined space between two buildings, with not more than four feet from wall to wall. He twisted and faced Delhi Road, glimpsing a truck bearing to the west.

Elmer was crouching against the opposite wall. "Can you lift that?" he inquired, and pointed at a manhole cover a yard to their rear.

"Where does it lead?" Hickok asked.

"Down into the sewers."

"We're not going down there?"

"We are if you want to find your friends," Elmer said.

Hickok sighed and edged to the cover. The rim was imbedded flush with the surface, but there was a single hole near the edge. He inserted his right index finger, rose to his knees, and heaved. The heavy metal lid rose a quarter of an inch.

"What's the matter, sonny? Are you a pansy?"

Gritting his teeth and straining his finger, hand, and arm, Hickok succeeded in elevating the manhole cover several inches. He gripped the rim with his left hand, bracing the lid, and jerked his finger from the hole.

"Don't drop it or we'll have the Commies breathing down our necks," Elmer said.

"Instead of flappin' your gums, why don't you lend me a hand?" Hickok queried.

"Since I'm the one with the brains, you can do all the heavy work."

Hickok eased the manhole cover aside and gently lowered it to the ground. "Tell me something, old-timer. Do you have many friends?"

"Very few."

"I figured as much."

"Most of them were killed by the Commies."

The gunman frowned, regretting he had baited the bum. "One day the Commies will get theirs," he stated to cover his embarrassment.

"I hope I'm around to see the day."

Hickok peered into the manhole and grimaced as a nauseating stench wafted upward. "I suppose there are cockroaches and rats down here too?"

"Tons of them."

"I knew it."

"But there are other things down there. Muties. We've got to stay on our toes every step of the way."

"Mutants, huh?"

"Yeah. I was told that a long, long time ago, right after the war, a lot of pink rain fell on the city. Many of the people were sick as dogs and a bunch died. They swept and flushed the rain into the sewer system, and ever since then there have been the Browns, the giant roaches, and other freaks of nature to deal with."

Pink rain? Was that the same thing as fallout? What color was radioactive fallout, anyway? Hickok pondered for a moment, staring into the murky cavity, spying metal rungs leading downward. "Do you go into the sewers very often?"

"Hardly ever. Too dangerous."

"I'll lead the way," Hickok offered.

"Thanks, sonny, but I will. I know which way to go and

what to look out for," Elmer said. "Besides, the lighter is mine." He produced his lighter from his left pants pocket and moved to the edge of the manhole, his countenance etched with anxiety.

"I can handle this myself," Hickok suggested. "Give me directions and I'll be okay."

Elmer looked at the gunman and grinned. "I promised to help you get into the L.R.F., and I'm a man of my word." With that, he slid his legs into the hole, twisting and grabbing the top metal rung.

"Be careful," Hickok said.

"You're the one who needs a nursemaid," Elmer responded, and lowered his body from view. A flickering glow filled the access hatch when he snapped on his lighter.

Admiring the oldster's gumption, Hickok angled his legs into the hole and clambered down the rungs. A narrow concrete walkway afforded footing at the bottom, and Hickok turned, the fetid, rancid odor almost making him gag.

Six feet high and six feet wide, the sewer tunnel was aligned from east to west. Between the walkway on which they stood, and a similar walkway on the other side, flowed a sluggish stream composed of reeking refuse, putrid garbage, and repulsive globs of indeterminate matter.

"That gunk is four feet deep," Elmer mentioned. "Don't fall in or you'll regret it."

"You don't have to tell me twice," Hickok said, revolted by the brownish sludge.

"This way," Elmer said, and headed to the east, treading carefully, the lighter held aloft in his right hand.

Hickok pinched his nose shut with his left hand and trailed after the bum.

"Keep your peepers on that crap," Elmer stated, and pointed at the sewage.

"Why?"

"The muties swim in the shit."

"You're kiddin' me."

"I wish I was."

How could anything exist in that sickening slime? Hickok stared at the festering muck, searching for a trace of life.

Elmer increased his pace, hastening at a rapid clip.

"What's your big hurry?" Hickok inquired, watching their shadows shift and undulate on the tunnel walls, concerned the old-timer might slip on the slick walkway.

"The sewer gives me the creeps."

"Wimp," Hickok joked, giving the bum a taste of his own medicine.

Elmer glanced at the sewage and hurried on.

They covered 30 yards uneventfully and came to a junction where another tunnel forked to the south.

"We go this way," Elmer said, and took the fork, his shoes padding on the cement. "This tunnel runs under Delhi Road. Sixty yards from here is one of the manholes on the L.R.F. grounds."

"So I'll come up inside the outer wall?" Hickok said.

"Wouldn't do you much good if you came up outside, now would it?"

"If you despise the sewers so much, how come you know about the tunnels into the L.R.F.?" Hickok asked.

"A pal of mine, Gorgeous George—"

"Gorgeous George?"

"Don't interrupt me, sonny," Elmer stated. "Gorgeous George and I were curious about the installation, and we wanted to take a look-see for ourselves. So one night we snuck down here and found this tunnel leading under the base. We scoped out the silver toothpick and other buildings and split before we were caught."

"Where's your pal now?"

"Gorgeous George bit the farm two months ago."

"I'm sorry to hear it."

"Was his own fault. The dummy got blitzed out of his gourd and passed out in a condemned building. He forgot to cover himself or curl into a ball and the rats got him. Chewed all the way through his throat."

"A horrible way to go," Hickok remarked.

"I can think of worse," Elmer said. "George should have . . ." he began, and halted abruptly. "What was that?"

Hickok stopped and listened, hearing the faint gurgling of the sewage and the dripping of sludge from the walls. "What?"

"Didn't you hear that noise?"

"Nope," Hickok responded.

Elmer shrugged and took a stride, then froze, extending the lighter over the sewage. "Damn it! Are you deaf?"

Hickok was about to tell the bum he was imagining things, until his ears registered the peculiar sound, like an indistinct swishing. Whatever it was, the sound came from their rear. "What is it?"

"A mutie!" Elmer exclaimed, casting a terrified glance backwards. "We've got to get the hell out of the sewer!" He spun and bolted as fast as his spindly legs would carry him.

Placing his right hand on his right Python, Hickok jogged on Elmer's heels, looking repeatedly at the tunnel behing them, alarmed that the swishing was becoming louder and louder.

"Oh, God! I hope we make it!" Elmer cried.

They traversed ten yards.

Hickok peered over his right shoulder again, and he felt as if his blood changed to ice as he beheld the sewage rippling and cresting with the passage under its surface of a large, sinuous . . .thing.

"Run!" Elmer screamed.

The mutant was on them in seconds.

Chapter Eighteen

Geronimo was 30 feet from the entrance to Lenin's Needle when he spied an open door to his left and darted through the doorway, hoping to find a stairwell, or weapons, or anything to turn the tide for the Warriors. Instead, he found a Russian trooper standing next to a rack containing cleaning supplies. In the trooper's hands was a broom.

"What are you doing, comrade?" the Russian inquired, his brown eyes narrowing.

"I thought this was the bathroom," Geronimo said, smiling, pivoting toward the door.

The soldier reached out and seized Geronimo by the right shoulder. "Wait a minute. There is something strange here."

"Your face," Geronimo responded, and batted the trooper's arm away. He lunged for the doorway, but the Russian leaped and tackled him about the ankles, bringing him down, sending him crashing into the open door and knocking it shut. Geronimo twisted onto his back, lashing his legs in an effort to dislodge the soldier.

The trooper clung to the Warrior and started to claw higher.

Eager to end the fray quickly and aid Blade, Geronimo reversed his strategy, arcing his knees up to his chest and drawing the soldier's face within range of his hands. He jammed his thumbs into the Russian's eyes, causing the man to cry out in pain, and slugged the trooper on the jaw.

Stunned, his eyes closed and watering, the soldier released his hold and tried to rise.

Geronimo flung his legs outward, ramming the Russian in the chest with the soles of his boots and hurling the trooper into the rack with a tremendous smash.

The soldier clutched at the rack for support, retaining his footing, and wiped at his eyes with his left sleeve.

Knowing every second was precious, Geronimo came off the floor in a rush, using his right shoulder as a battering ram and plowing into the man's midsection. Grunting, the trooper doubled over, and Geronimo drove his head upward, catching the soldier on the tip of the chin and mashing the Russian's teeth together. Geronimo delivered two blows to the man's abdomen, anticipating an easy victory, but the trooper was hardier than he thought.

With a wicked snap of his body, the soldier kneed the Warrior in the groin.

Lancing agony speared through Geronimo and he backed off, his hands spread protectively over his privates.

Relentlessly the Russian closed in, boxing his foe on the right cheek, then the left.

Geronimo reeled and tottered to the right. He brought up his arms to defend himself as the trooper pounced and they both toppled to the floor, grappling and flailing.

Somewhere in the distance the sound of gunfire arose.

Blade must be in trouble!

Energized by a surge of adrenaline, Geronimo butted his forehead into the Russian's nose, crushing the cartilage, blood spraying on his face. He held the fingers of his right hand rigid and struck the soldier in the throat.

Uttering a protracted gasp, the Russian clasped his hands

to his neck and scrambled on his back away from the Warrior.
He bumped into the rack of supplies and pushed to his knees.

Geronimo pressed his advantage, rolling onto his left side
and aiming a kick at the trooper's head.

The Russian managed to block the Warrior's leg.

Undaunted, Geronimo attacked, setting upon the soldier with
a rain of Hung Gar hand blows taught to him by a Family
Elder skilled in the martial arts. The trooper deflected several,
and then Geronimo hit home with a tiger claw to the jaw, a
leopard paw to the Adam's apple, and a dragon fist to the
mouth.

Dazed and breathing in deep gulps of air, spittle on his lower
lip and blood seeping from the corners of his mouth, the
Russian slumped to the floor and began twitching convulsively.

Geronimo rose, his knees a bit unsteady, pain still flaring
in his groin. He stepped toward the door, gathering his
strength, listening for the chattering of automatic weapons.

All was quiet outside the utility closet.

Rendered careless by his anxiety over Blade and the torment,
Geronimo yanked on the doorknob and took a stride into the
corridor—and immediately regretted his rashness.

"We meet again, Warrior," General Ari Stoljarov declared
sarcastically.

Geronimo frowned, seething with frustration. The Butcher
stood four feet to his left, and flanking the general were two
guards with their AK-47's at the ready.

"I heard a commotion in the closet and stopped to
investigate," General Stoljarov said. He walked to the
doorway and gazed in at the trooper, who was now lying still
with his tongue protruding. "Ahhhhh. I see. You two were
arguing over who would sweep the floor."

"Up yours," Geronimo snapped.

General Stoljarov looked at the Warrior, his eyebrows
arching. "Where is your vaunted humor now, Indian?"

Geronimo glared but said nothing.

"My men are in pursuit of Blade, and I expect he will be
apprehended at any moment," Stoljarov said.

"Dream on. You won't catch Blade twice. He'll take your men apart," Geronimo predicted.

General Stoljarov scratched his chin, contemplating. "Perhaps you are right," he agreed with a smirk and strolled to a point ten feet farther along the opposite wall. Adorning the wall at shoulder height was a square black box, each side four inches in length, and situated in the center of the box was a red button. "Perhaps my men will require assistance," he declared, and depressed the button.

Lenin's Needle abruptly resounded to the harsh blaring of a multitude of klaxons.

The Butcher returned to Geronimo and grinned, raising his voice to be heard above the din. "Now how far do you think your friend will get? The alarm I've sounded will place everyone in the Needle on alert, and our security personnel will conduct a sweep of every floor."

"You won't stop Blade."

General Stoljarov snorted. "I'd expect such misguided loyalty from you. Despite his formidable reputation, Blade is human, after all. Even he can not hope to withstand my troops." He motioned with his right arm. "After you."

"Where are you taking me?" Geronimo asked, moving forward.

The guards diligently kept their AK-47's pointed at the Warrior and fell in behind him.

"I thought you might enjoy meeting Leonid Grineva," General Stoljarov said, heading down the hall on Geronimo's right.

"The scientist who developed your superweapon?" Geronimo responded suspiciously.

"Yes."

"Why?"

"Alpha Triad has traveled so far to learn the secret of our new weapon," General Stoljarov replied. "The least I can do is alleviate your curiosity."

"Why?"

"Has anyone ever told you that you're paranoid?" Stoljarov

queried, and laughed.

What was the Butcher up to? Geronimo wondered as they came to a junction and took the left-hand passage. Leonid Grineva should be the *last* person Stoljarov would want either of the Warriors to meet. If Grineva's brilliant intellect truly was responsible for the creation of the L.R.F., then under no circumstances should the general be willing to expose the scientist to potential danger. And Stoljarov must know that the Warriors would terminate Grineva if given the opportunity.

In 40 yards they came to an elevator, and General Stoljarov pushed the UP button. He eyed Geronimo smugly. When the door hissed open, he gestured for the Warrior to step inside, then entered with the guards. The soldiers held the AK-47 barrels within an inch of the Warrior's head, and the general punched a numbered button on the control panel. The door closed.

"I hope you're not afraid of heights," Stoljarov said.

"Are we going all the way up to the crystal globe?" Geronimo inquired. He could feel a slight vibration in the floor as the elevator ascended.

"No. The crystal globe is actually part of the laser's firing apparatus, as I understand it. The inner surface of the crystal is coated with silver to reflect almost all of the light generated inside the crystal," Stoljarov revealed. "We are on our way to the control room, which is directly under the crystal."

The elevator climbed swiftly, the number of each respective level lighting on the control panel to mark their progress.

"Are you willing to cooperate with me and spare yourself extreme discomfort?" General Stoljarov asked.

"Cooperate?" Geronimo repeated.

"I've been giving the matter some consideration, and I've decided to question you before contacting General Malenkov," the Butcher disclosed. "You were right. I do want to impress Comrade Malenkov, and the way to do so is by obtaining information he dearly desires. He has long wanted to know the precise layout of your Home, and as much information as can be gleaned about every member of your Family, particularly the Elders and those Warriors about whom we know very little." He paused and pursed his lips. "Your capture will impress General Malenkov, but I could impress him even more if I obtain the information he needs. Imagine the boost to my career if I break you down and elicit the intelligence data Malenkov has been unable to obtain."

"Don't count your stars before they're pinned on."

"The irony of this is that the information is no longer essential. General Malenkov has wanted to learn the weaknesses of the Home in order to destroy your accursed Family. Some of our officers have proposed using a helicopter squadron, but the Home is too far from our lines for our helicopters to fly there and back without the necessity of refueling. A missile strike was suggested, but our long-range missiles are not as reliable as we would wish, and without a nuclear warhead, which we don't have, our missiles are incapable of delivering a payload that would obliterate your thirty-acre compound. General Malenkov does not want any survivors, any martyrs who would rouse the Freedom Federation to avenge our deed."

The elevator passed the fifteenth floor.

"Once Comrade Grineva has demonstrated the laser can be used against land targets," General Stoljarov continued, "we won't need any information other than the Home's location, which we already know. Grineva will feed the coordinates into the computer firing system, and the laser will vaporize the Home like it did the 757."

Vaporize the Home! The idea that the Family could be incinerated without warning from a thousand miles away horrified Geronimo. His loved ones and friends would never know what hit them. The scenario of long-distance annihilation was new to him. He'd read about the prewar civilization, how the ordinary citizen never knew when he or she might be subjected to an extraordinary death by nuclear incineration, how the prospect of imminent doom hung over their heads like an ominous cloud. Was this the same experience? Knowing that someone, somewhere, possessed the means of wiping out everyone you loved at the touch of a button? The reality rocked him to his core.

"General Malenkov himself will undoubtedly want to be the one who fires the laser at your Home. The eradication of the Family is a pet project of his, you know," General Stoljarov said.

Geronimo scarcely paid attention, his mind racing with the implications of the Butcher's revelations. This meant that the Home would never be safe. Even if the Warriors succeeded in demolishing Lenin's Needle, there was no guarantee someone else at sometime in the future wouldn't develop another scheme, wouldn't construct another deadly device. His wife and son, his beloved Cynthia and Cochise, would never truly be safe.

"Do you know what a satellite is?" General Stoljarov inquired.

"What?" Geronimo responded absently.

"A satellite. A man-made device launched into orbit around the earth. The U.S. and the U.S.S.R. were sending satellites into orbit constantly before the war, and many of those satellites were used exclusively by the military establishments in both countries. Two years ago we discovered one of the Soviet war satellites was still in orbit, and we now use that satellite in our laser-guidance system. Lenin's Needle is actually an enormous laser, and the laser light is generated and amplified here. We direct the beam at our satellite, and the satellite, which was once incorporated into the Soviet anti-satellite laser network, deflects the beam to any spot we select. In conjuction with our computer and our E.R.T.E., our Extended Radar Tracking Equipment, we can hit any target within fifteen hundred miles of Cincinnati."

"I had no idea the Russians were such cowards," Geronimo stated.

"You dare call us cowards?"

"You would rather destroy us from afar than take us on face-to-face," Geronimo noted.

"Spare me your juvenile morality. We have developed a

flawless system of laser warfare, and we would be fools not to employ our laser against our enemies. Our method is not based on cowardice, but expediency. Rather than suffer through a sustained conflict with the Federation and our other enemies, we will defeat them in a tenth of the time conventional forces would require. Eventually, once we've extended the laser's range, we'll subjugate the world.''

"I'm getting tired of listening to your bragging," Geronimo mentioned.

"You won't need to listen to me much longer," General Stoljarov said. "We've arrived."

The elevator slowed to a stop and the door widened, revealing a huge chamber containing sophisticated electronic equipment; consoles, monitors, banks, and sundry cabinets crammed the room. A dozen or more technicians, all wearing red smocks, were seated at various chairs. Sitting at a large control console five yards from the elevator was a short, skinny man with a bald head and wire-rimmed glasses. He turned as the elevator arrived and nodded at the Butcher.

"General Stoljarov. Are you aware the security alarm has been activated?"

"Yes, Comrade Grineva. I was the one who activated it," the general said, advancing to the console.

The guards nudged Geronimo with their AK-47's, prodding him forward.

"I took the liberty of shutting off the speakers in the Control Room. We could not concentrate with so much noise."

"How is the work proceeding?" General Stoljarov asked.

"We are making headway. I expect to be ready for the land-target test within twenty-four hours," Grineva replied, and squinted at the Warrior. "Who is this?"

"His name is Geronimo."

"Why have you brought him here?"

"I'll explain in a moment," Stoljarov said, and moved to a telephone on the left side of the console. He scooped up the receiver and pressed the number nine. "Colonel Zaitsev, this is General Stoljarov. Yes, I know. I did. Two of my men are guarding the north exit, and the south exit should have been locked after the day shift departed. There is an intruder in the Needle, the Warrior known as Blade. What? You have? And all the floors are being swept? Excellent. I'm in the Control Room. Notify me the moment you have him in custody." He hung up and glanced at his prisoner, smiling. "Our security people plan to set a trap for Blade on the tenth floor."

"Are you sure it's not the other way around?" Geronimo quipped.

Stoljarov straightened and looked at Grineva. "Is the Booth available?"

Leonid Grineva did a double take. "The Booth? Yes, but why would . . ." he began, and stared at Geronimo. "No!"

"Yes," General Stoljarov said.

"But the Booth is meant to be used for research," Grineva protested. "It's where I work on my theories and try to solve problems."

"I am in charge of this facility, am I not?" Stoljarov queried.

"Yes, but—"

"Then I can utilize the Booth as I see fit," the Butcher declared, and snapped his fingers at the guards.

"To the right," one of the soldiers directed Geronimo.

"This is most improper," Grineva commented.

Geronimo walked to the right, past a wide cabinet, and spotted a door in the far corner of the room. A barrel poked him in the small of the back, and he strolled nonchalantly to the door, determined to deprive the Butcher of the satisfaction of seeing him betray any fear.

General Stoljarov stepped past the Warrior, opened the door, and switched on an overhead light. Within the room was a metal table five feet in length. On the opposite end of the table rested a strange rectangular device hooked to a six-foot-high bank of apparatuses displaying a score of dials, knobs, and switches. The top and sides of the rectangular device were gray, and the right side sported four dials and a switch. Aligned toward the end of the table nearest the door was the front of the device, a black panel with a circular hole in the center.

"This model is one of Grineva's early experimental versions," General Stoljarov disclosed, moving to the rectangular device and patting its top. "To him it's a tool to be used to further his knowledge. To me it's a toy to be used for my pleasure." He reached under the table and produced a ten-inch length of steel plate. "Take this," he ordered the taller of the two guards.

The soldier obeyed promptly.

"Hold the plate at the end of the table," Stoljarov instructed. "Make certain the plate is in line with the hole."

Geronimo and the second trooper stepped to the left as the tall soldier came around the table and held the steel plate away from his body, his fingers at the very edge.

"This is not a very powerful model," Stoljarov said. "But it will suffice. Now watch. I've seen Grineva do this many times, and he even gave me a lesson once." He flicked the switch and rotated the uppermost dial, and the rectangular device began to hum loudly. A pinpoint of light became visible in the hole in the black panel.

The tall soldier gazed anxiously at the laser, apparently nervous about the fate of his fingers.

"Here goes," Stoljarov declared, and turned the second dial.

A pencil-thin beam of red light shot from the hole and struck the steel plate in the middle. The tall soldier flinched but kept the plate steady. Wisps of smoke spiraled upward and a crackling and sizzling arose. Sparks flew. An acrid scent filled the room.

General Stoljarov unexpectedly turned the laser off. "That's enough of a demonstration."

The tall soldier breathed an audible sigh of relief and lowered the plate to the table.

"Comrade Grineva made a major breakthrough in the generation of the beam," the general said. "We can widen the laser light to encompass the target, whether the target is the size of a 747 or a car. We can't enlarge it enough to incinerate the Home with one blast, but ten or twelve computer-directed blasts should do the trick."

"You bastard," Geronimo stated.

With a wicked sneer, the Butcher motioned at the two troopers. "Restrain his arms."

The tall soldier covered Geronimo while the second trooper leaned his AK-47 against the wall and gripped the Warrior's wrists.

"Both of you," General Stoljarov directed. "Hold him securely."

"Close your eyes," the tall soldier ordered Geronimo.

The Warrior complied, and the next moment each arm was seized by one of the Russians.

"Open them."

Geronomi did, to see the tall soldier's AK-47 propped against the right side of the table and to find the tall soldier clutching his right arm and the second man his left.

"Position him at the end of the table," General Stoljarov commanded.

The guards roughly hauled him into place.

"And now the fun can begin," stated the Butcher. "I want his face in line with the hole."

Geronimo knew what was coming next. He struggled, striving to break free, but the soldiers forced him to bend over, applying excruciating pressure to his arms. He looked up and stared directly into the hole in the laser.

The Butcher leaned forward, his hands on the table. "And now you will tell me everything I want to know, or little by little, bit by bit, I will burn the flesh from your head."

Chapter Nineteen

Blade never hesitated, never broke stride. He was on the six-man squad in three bounds, ramming the stock of the AK-47 into the mouth of the first soldier and dropping the next with a fierce swipe to the side of the man's head. Whipping to the right, he smashed his right elbow against the nose of a third adversary, then planted his left combat boot in the groin of the fourth. Only then did he employ the AK-47, firing two shots, one apiece into each remaining Russian's forehead. He scanned the writhing, groaning figures on the floor and took off.

Where could Geronimo be?

In 20 feet he came to a door with two words stenciled in black letters on the panel. The top word was STAIRWELL, and the one underneath was in another language with strange lettering, undoubtedly Russian. He tested the knob, elated to discover the door was unlocked, and left the corridor. As the door closed he heard a commotion to his rear; General Stoljarov's men must have found the six-man squad.

Move! his mind shrieked.

Blade took the stairs three at a stride. He reached a landing and continued higher, deliberating his next move. Being separated from Hickok and Geronimo compounded his problem. It wasn't enough that he had the superweapon and the Hurricane to worry about. Now he had to find his friends. This mission, like most of those in the past, had evolved into a fiasco. No matter how hard he tried, how much he planned, something always went wrong. Always.

Murphy strikes again.

He came to another landing and went higher, wanting to put as much distance as possible between Stoljarov's men and himself. He expected an alarm to sound at any moment, and once it did everyone in Lenin's Needle would be on the alert. With his ill-fitting uniform, he would undoubtedly stick out like the proverbial sore thumb. How many people, he wondered, occupied the building after the day shift went home? A skeleton crew?

A third landing appeared, and still he climbed.

What was his first priority? Locating his fellow Warriors was important, but putting the silver spire out of commission was imperative. There must be a control room, and logic dictated it would be on an upper floor. Wrecking the control room, then, should be his primary goal.

Hickok and Geronimo would have to wait.

Blade was almost to the next landing when klaxons went off, reverberating in the stairwell, creating a raucous clamor. He went to the door and peeked out.

A pair of troopers were walking down a wide corridor, their backs to the stairwell. They halted at a closed door 40 feet away, and one of them cautiously thrust the door inward. Their AK-47's in their hands, they darted from view.

Blade was out of the stairwell in a flash, running to a door on the left and boldly entering the room beyond to find four rows of long metal tables covered with beakers, flasks, and Bunsen burners. A chemical laboratory? What use would the Soviets have for a chemical lab? He peered into the hall.

A trooper came into view at the far end, carrying objects and strolling in the direction of the chemical lab.

Blade's gray eyes narrowed. There was something familiar about the items the man transported, and it took several seconds for the shape of two articles in the soldier's right hand to register: the Bowies! And there was the Commando, slung over the Russian's left shoulder. Geronimo's SAR dangled from the trooper's right shoulder, and in his right hand he bore the Arminius and the tomahawk.

What was the soldier doing with them?

Resolving to reclaim his weapons at any cost, Blade watched the trooper enter a room 60 feet distant. He was tempted to make a dash to the room, but the thought of the pair of Russians in the other chamber deterred him. He would need to get past them without being detected.

The solitary trooper reappeared and strolled away, exiting through a door on the right-hand side.

One problem disposed of.

Blade patiently bided his time, wishing the klaxons would cease caterwauling. A minute later the duo materialized. They closed the door behind them and walked farther away, to the adjacent room, involved in a conversation Blade couldn't hear because of the din.

The klaxons.

If he couldn't hear the troopers, they wouldn't be able to hear him.

Blade stared at their backs, took a breath, and charged, his long legs flying, covering six feet at a spring, his finger on the AK-47 trigger just in case they turned.

Neither so much as suspected his presence.

. With a final leap Blade was behind them, clubbing one with the stock, the second with the barrel. Both stumbled and fell to their knees, and he struck each man again, knocking them senseless. A glance in both directions insured there were no witnesses. Blade slung the AK-47 over his left arm, then crouched and draped an unconscious Russian over each broad shoulder. His massive leg muscles quivered as he rose and hurried toward the room where the weapons had been stashed.

If soldiers emerged from any of the rooms now, he'd be at their mercy.

Blade reached the door and attempted to turn the knob, frowning when he discovered it was locked. He stepped back, clasped the Russians firmly, and delivered a kick with his right boot, his steely sinews snapping the lock, splitting the jamb, and causing the door to fly inward. He entered, groped for a light switch, and flicked on the light, then lowered the soldiers to the floor. As he shut the door he surveyed the chamber, noting a row of metal lockers lined against the rear wall, a rack of AK-47's on the left wall and, of all things, a blackboard on the right.

What was the reason for the blackboard?

In the center of the room stood two tables piled with weapons and gear, and there, on the top of the nearest heap, were the Bowies in their sheaths. Blade let the AK-47 fall and crossed to the table. A garment in another pile caught his attention, and he suddenly realized all of their clothing, evidently taken from the jeep, lay in a jumbled bundle.

He looked down at himself, at the ludicrous uniform, and, in a fit of annoyance, took hold of the front of his shirt, his brawny hands bunching the fabric, and yanked his arms outward, popping every button. Working swiftly, he removed the Soviet uniform and donned his green fatigue pants, the leather vest, and his Bowies. Why bother wearing the Russian uniform anymore? he reasoned. Every soldier at the L.R.F. must be aware that the Warriors were on the premises, so the uniform had lost its value as a disguise. Besides, he was tired of feeling cramped and uncomfortable. If he had to take on the Russian Army, then he would confront them in his own clothes. He patted his pants pockets, verifying the spare ammo was still there.

Almost ready.

Blade slung Geronimo's SAR over his left shoulder, and tucked the tomahawk under his belt next to his left Bowie. He placed the Arminius in the small of his back, then paused.

What should he do about Hickok's buckskins and gunbelt, Geronimo's shoulder holster and clothes, and their moccasins?

He walked to the row of dull green metal lockers and opened one in the center.

Bingo.

The locker contained a brown backpack, a web belt with a survival knife attached, a Russian helmet, and a uniform shirt. He went from locker to locker, finding indentical gear in every one. Were these storage lockers for some of the troops? He took a backpack from the last locker and returned to the table, taking but a few seconds to cram everything inside, then donned the pack. Satisfied, he stepped to the door, threw it wide, and stalked into the corridor.

And walked right into trouble.

A trio of soldiers stood 20 feet to the right, their AK-47's at their sides, in the act of advancing down the hall, their expressions reflecting their bewilderment at his abrupt appearance.

Blade shot them. He whipped the Commando from right to left, the heavy slugs tearing into the troopers and slamming them to the floor with their chests perforated, their bodies racked by spasms. Since he knew additional Russians would be coming up the stairwell after him, he opted to wheel to the left and head for the end of the corridor. Only then did he realize the klaxons had stopped wailing.

Someone must have heard the Commando.

So what?

He hadn't gone ten yards when he saw the elevator and halted in front of the door. The numbers overhead indicated the car was on its way down. Good. He pushed the button and surveyed the corridor.

No reinforcements yet.

In 15 seconds the elevator arrived, the door sliding open to reveal two officers, each of whom wore a pistol in a belt holster.

"What the hell!" the older of the pair blurted.

Blade sent several rounds into the older officer's face, the impact hurling the Russian against the rear of the car. He collapsed at the feet of the younger officer, who seemed to be in a state of shock.

"Do you know who I am?" Blade asked harshly, moving into the elevator and touching the tip of the Commando barrel to the officer's forehead.

"Yes," the man exclaimed, gulping.

"And you must know about the Hurricane out front."

"Yes," the officer said.

"And here's the question that determines whether you live or die," Blade informed him. "I know the pilot survived, and I suspect he's being forced to teach your pilots about our VTOL. Where is he?"

The officer licked his lips. "The seventh floor," he divulged quickly. "He's being held on the seventh floor."

"Congratulations. You get to live."

"Thanks," the officer responded weakly.

Blade hit the button for the seventh floor, and then hit the young officer squarely on the jaw with his left fist, his shoulder and arm muscles rippling, crumpling the hapless Russian. "But I never said I'd leave you in one piece," he commented, and unslung the SAR.

The elevator reached the seventh floor an instant later.

With the Commando in his right hand and the SAR in his left, Blade emerged into a hornet's nest of Russian soldiers. He cut loose ambidextrously, firing in both directions, taking the Soviets completely unawares, the stocks of both weapons clamped under his armpits to absorb the recoil. There were too many troopers to bother counting them; he simply mowed them down in droves, their death wails and screams commingling in an eerie chorus. His withering hail of lead caught those foolish enough to rush from various rooms upon hearing the thundering of his weapons. Only when the SAR went empty did he cease firing.

Crimson-splattered figures littered the corridor, many moaning and contorting in anguish.

Blade tilted his head and shouted at the top of his lungs.

"Captain Stuart! Captain Lyle Stuart! Can you hear me? This is Blade!"

A muffled cry came from a door 20 feet to the right.

Alert for the merest hint of hostility, Blade threaded a path over and between the corpses and the wounded and halted next to the door. "Captain Stuart?" He slung the SAR over his left shoulder.

"Blade? Is it really you? The door is locked."

"Stand back," Blade advised. He executed a snap kick to the wood near the knob, and there was a resounding crack and the door popped open.

A lean, handsome man attired in the blue uniform of a pilot in the Free State of California Air Force stepped into view, limping on his left leg. His features were haggard and pale, but his green eyes were lively and radiating happiness. "I never expected to see you again!" he exclaimed. "I can't believe you came for me!"

"Save the celebrating for later," Blade said. "Can you walk?"

"The leg was fractured when these sons of bitches brought me down," Lyle disclosed. "It's pretty much healed. I'll keep up. Don't worry."

"Then grab an AK-47 and stick by my side," Blade stated.

Lyle shuffled into the hall and took an assault rifle from a slain soldier. "Are you here alone?"

"Hickok and Geronimo are with me, sort of," Blade replied.

"Sort of?"

"We can't stay on this floor," Blade said, heading for the elevator. "The Russians will throw everyone they have at us now. Do you know where the control room is located?"

"On the twenty-fifth floor."

"Then that's where we're going," Blade declared. He stopped suddenly, staring at the oval metal object clutched in the hand of a dead Russian officer.

"What is it?" Lyle asked nervously, his view obstructed by the giant's body.

"Hand grenade," Blade answered, and leaned down, rummaging through the officer's pockets. He found two more grenades, and stuffed all three into his own pants. "Let's go."

They hastened into the elevator and the Warrior pressed the button for the 25th floor.

Lyle leaned against the rear wall as the car rose, grinning and shaking his head. "I just can't believe this is really happening."

"Believe it."

"You have no idea of the hell I've been through. The commander here, a bastard by the name of Stoljarov, used electroshock torture to persuade me to teach the Soviets about the Hurricane."

"I gathered as much."

"I've been holding back," Lyle said. "They don't know as much as they think they do."

"Can you fly the Hurricane?" Blade queried.

"No problem."

"You may get your chance," Blade said.

Without warning the elevator jerked to a sharp stop, nearly causing both men to lose their balance, and the lights went out.

"What's happening?" Lyle asked.

Blade looked at the control panel, which was also unlit, and scowled. "We're stuck on about the tenth floor."

"Why?"

"Three guesses," Blade replied.

A booming voice addressed them from the other side of the door. "Attention, you in the elevator! We have cut your power and demand your immediate surrender!"

"What do we do?" the pilot whispered.

Blade slung the Commando over his right arm and fished the grenades from his pockets. "Take one," he directed, handing it over. "Don't pull the pin until I give the word."

"Did you hear me?" the voice outside barked.

"I heard you," Blade responded.

"Then you will lay any weapons on the floor and raise your arms over your head. We will open the door at the count of three. If you have not complied, you will be shot.''

Blade leaned toward the captain. "They'll need to restore the power to the elevator to open the door. Get set."

"One!" the Russian called out gruffly.

"They don't know there are two of us in here," Blade mentioned. "Are they in for a surprise. Stand to the left of the door."

"Two!"

Blade stepped to the right, inserting a finger into the circular ring of each grenade.

"Three!" the voice shouted.

"Now!" Blade whispered, and jerked both pins out.

The lights came on abruptly, and a second later the door started to slide open.

Blade knew the timing was critical. At the instant there was just enough space for the grenade to fit through the opening, he nodded at Lyle. They tossed their grenades into the corridor in unison, and Blade immediately stabbed the button for the 25th floor.

"Grenades!" someone in the hall screeched. "Grenades!"

Blade flattened against the side of the elevator, his eyes riveted to the door. Would it open all the way or swing shut? Would one of the Russians fire into the elevator, or were the troopers all too busy scrambling for cover? Would the elevator withstand the explosion, or would they be crushed to death or plummet to the bottom of the shaft? All of these thoughts raced through his mind, and then the door was closing again and the elevator started upward. If the grenades were typical, there would be a ten-second delay between the pulling of the pins and the detonation. At least five seconds had already elapsed, and he mentally ticked off the remaining five as the elevator rose rapidly, passing the 11th floor and almost reaching the 12th.

The blast was tremendous.

The elevator bounced and swayed as if it were being shaken by an invisible giant. Blade and Lyle Stuart were buffeted from side to side, smacking into the walls repeatedly, jouncing every which way. The elevator heaved and tilted, falling and rising, before finally stabilizing, coming to rest in an upright position with the lights still on.

Lyle was on his back in the right-hand corner. He gazed in wonder at the door and the lights. "We're alive!" he breathed. "We've alive!"

But they weren't moving.

Blade wound up near the rear, his hands against the wall. He stepped to the panel and punched the button for the 25th floor several times. "Come on!" he prompted. "Don't fail us now!"

With a grinding lurch, the elevator resumed its ascent.

"We did it!" Lyle said, rising to his feet unsteadily.

Blade unslung the Commando and faced the door. "We're not out of the woods yet."

Chapter Twenty

Hickok could scarcely credit his own eyes.

The mutant surging out of the sewer was an enormous, repulsive, leechlike creature with glistening greenish-brown skin divided into segmented rings and a huge, disk-shaped maw. Slimy refuse sprayed in all directions as the mutant broke the surface and reared like a striking cobra.

'No!'' Elmer cried, fear lending speed to his legs.

Hickok slowed, the right Python streaking from under his shirt. He snapped off three shots from the hip, and all three hit home, drilling into the mutant's body. The booming of the Colt was deafening.

Stung by the slugs, the leech veered past the Warrior and bore down on the bum.

"Elmer!" Hickok yelled. "Look out!" He sprinted forward, attempting to reach Elmer's side before the leech attacked.

The mutant got there first.

Elmer's feet were pumping frantically when his right heel made contact with a wad of slippery sewage on the walkway and he fell, his arms swinging wildly, landing on his buttocks.

Hickok saw the leech angle down and in, its huge mouth fastening on Elmer's face, choking off his strangled scream, the disk covering Elmer from his hairline to his chin.

"Try me!" Hickok cried, thumbing the hammer twice, each shot smacking into the center of the creature's thick body.

Oblivious to its wounds, the leech whipped its body backward, dragging Elmer with it, his arms and legs thrashing, causing the lighter to flicker out and plunging the tunnel into dank darkness. The mutant's inky bulk was barely visible as it dived into the sewage, its mouth gripping Elmer's face with the power of a vise, hauling the flailing bum under the surface.

"Elmer!" Hickok shouted, taking several paces and halting, shocked by the sudden demise of his newfound friend. Except for a faint swishing, the tunnel was quiet. Goose bumps broke out all over his body as he gazed at the foul, black stream.

Dear Spirit!

Elmer was gone!

And the gunman realized he could well be next. Without the feeble light cast by the lighter, he was shrouded in gloom. If another leech should come after him, he'd have scant warning. And as it was, the Pythons were ineffective against the bloodsucking worms. He replaced the right Colt under his shirt.

There was only one thing to do.

Head for the hills.

So to speak.

Hickok hastened along the tunnel, staying as close to the wall as he could, straining his ears to hear the telltale swishing of the leeches.

How many yards before he reached the access tunnel?

The gunman frowned, thinking of Elmer, wishing he could have saved the poor man. He'd only known Elmer for a short while, but he'd grown to like the old-timer. His failure to protect his newfound companion distressed him terribly. As a Warrior, his whole life was devoted to safeguarding others, whether they belonged to the Family or not. Rarely had he let those he was protecting down, making Elmer's death all the harder to take. The man had tried to help him, had saved him from the Russians, and he had flopped when Elmer needed him the most. There was no one else he could blame. The responsibility belonged to him.

And the Soviets.

Elmer would still be alive if not for the Russian super-weapon. Without the development of the L.R.F., the Warriors would not have traveled to Cincinnati, and Elmer would not have offered to help.

Yes, sir.

Any way Hickok considered the circumstances, the ultimate blame had to be shared with the Commies, and the longer he dwelled on Elmer's horrid end, the angrier he became. He covered 30 yards immersed in cogitation.

What was that?

Hickok drew up short as an indistinct swishing sounded from the rear. He looked back, the hair at the nape of his neck prickling.

Another leech!

Or maybe the same mutant returning for a second helping!

The gunman turned and raced recklessly on the cement. Never again would he wear someone else's footwear! The boots he'd taken from one of the dead troopers fit too tightly, cramping his feet, slowing him down. He could hear the swishing growing louder, and he sensed the leech was after him. His eyes detected a break in the tunnel ahead, a lighter shading near the top, and he ran for all he was worth.

The swishing seemed to be right on his heels.

Hickok reached the patch of feeble light and glanced up, perceiving the outline of a manhole cover and the metal rungs leading upward. There was a hiss almost in his ear, and he leaped into the air, his outstretched fingers catching on a rung as something nipped at his right foot. He banged against the side, then climbed quickly, applying his right shoulder to the lid and heaving. The cover slid partially aside, and he grabbed the edge with his right hand and shoved.

There was a commotion in the sewer below.

The gunman clambered from the hole and rolled to the right, and he heard a heavy body slap the rim and then a loud splash. Inhaling the fresh air deep into his lungs, Hickok rose to his knees, finding himself in the middle of a deserted, narrow side street.

He'd made it!

But his relief was fleeting. The gunman stood and proceeded to load the spent chambers in his right Python.

So much for the leeches.

Now he had a score to settle with the Russians.

But wasn't that the way it always was? There were always scores to settle. A death for a death. Tit for tat. And there were always those innocents who wound up caught in the crossfire.

The thought gave him pause.

Chapter Twenty-one

The Butcher reached out and patted the top of the laser. "Perhaps I should start with one of your ears," he said, and grinned.

Geronimo looked at the small hole through which the laser beam would be fired, and tensed. The two soldiers had his stocky body bent at the waist, with his shoulders and head above the tabletop. His arms were twisted up and back, and his sockets ached terribly.

"Move his head to the left," General Stoljarov ordered.

The tall trooper gripped Geronimo's chin in his right hand and pushed, but Geronimo jerked his head away.

"Not like that, imbecile!" the Butcher snapped. "Move his entire body."

By increasing the pressure on his arms to compel compliance, the soldiers sidled their captive to the left.

"Now hold his head steady," Stoljarov instructed.

Again the tall trooper grasped the Warrior's chin.

General Stoljarov leaned down, gauging the alignment, and

motioned at the tall guard. "Your body is too close to his ear. You're in my line of fire."

The trooper stepped back, arching his spine to ensure his abdomen was out of the beam's projected path.

"So what will it be?" the Butcher asked Geronimo. "Will you sketch the complete layout of the Home for me?"

"Give me a pencil—" Geronimo said.

General Stoljarov smiled in triumph.

"—and I'll shove it up your ass," Geronimo finished.

The Butcher frowned, his eyes narrowing. "Very well. You have brought this on yourself. I've heard many stories about how brave the Warriors are supposed to be. Now let's put your bravery to the test." He adjusted the dials, then smirked. "This will hurt you more than it will me."

Geronimo focused on the second dial, the one the Butcher would turn to activate the laser. He must make his move the moment *before* the dial was rotated. His best hope lay in grabbing the AK-47 propped against the right side of the table, and first he had to break free of the guards. The trooper on the left stood in a firm stance and would be difficult to dislodge, but the tall soldier on the right was standing awkwardly. Geronimo tensed his legs, his eyes on the laser.

"After I burn a hole in your ear, I think I'll work on your forehead," General Stoljarov said.

Geronimo said nothing.

"Have you ever smelled burning flesh?" the Butcher asked, and touched the second dial.

Concentrate on those fingers! Geronimo told himself. He saw the fingertips grip the dial and start to turn, and he threw himself to the left, against the shorter trooper, while yanking his right arm downward, feeling as if he tore every muscle in his arm. The unexpected tactic took the tall guard by surprise and he was pulled off balance, directly in line with the laser at the distant the red beam flared.

The tall soldier uttered a petrified shriek as the beam seared into his groin, flaming through his pants and underwear and scorching his gonads. He released Geronimo and stumbled backwards, automatically lowering his hands over his genitals, and cried out when the laser burned off two of his fingers.

Geronimo wrenched his right arm loose and pivoted, driving his fist into the short guard's stomach, then extended his right thumb and spiked it straight up, burying the digit in the fleshy folds of the man's throat. The hold on his left arm slackened, and he dove for the floor, tearing his left arm from the trooper's grasp, and scrambled to the right side of the table. He surged erect, his hands closing on the AK-47 and sweeping the gun to his right shoulder.

The tall Russian was staring down at himself in terror as the laser penetrated his body, while the short soldier gurgled and wheezed, his features livid. Only the Butcher saw the Warrior grab the weapon, and he reacted by taking hold of the laser and attempting to swivel the device at the Indian.

Geronimo shot Stoljarov first, smiling as he squeezed the trigger, seeing the Butcher's head dissolve into chunks and pieces of flesh and hair. He spun, the next rounds slamming into the short soldier's chest and flinging him against the wall.

Bubbling blood out his mouth, the tall Russian was sinking slowly to the floor, the red beam slicing his torso up the center, splitting him in half.

Shooting him would be a waste of ammunition, Geronimo decided, and ran for the door, skirting the dying soldier. He entered the Control Room, heading for the elevator, and shot a pair of technicians on a console to his right, then a third man in red seated at a computer to his left.

"Look out!" a woman yelled.

"Get down!" bellowed another.

Geronimo advanced toward the elevator, shooting any technicians foolish enough to show themselves, and when he was within ten yards of the elevator door he began firing at the equipment, reducing a bank of complicated instuments and panels to smoldering, sparking ruins.

"No! Don't!"

Geronimo stopped, staring at the skinny man with the wire-rimmed glasses coming toward him down an aisle on the right.

"You don't realize what you're doing!" Leonid Grineva declared. "This is a work of a lifetime!"

His lips compressing, Geronimo trained the AK-47 on the scientist.

Leonid Grineva blinked rapidly and extended his arms, palms out. "Wait! You can't!"

"Watch me," Geronimo said.

"But I was just doing my job!" Grineva declared.

"So am I," Geronimo responded, and stitched the genius from his navel to his neck. Without a backward glance he walked to the elevator and went to press the button.

The door opened.

"Going down?"

Geronimo's mouth dropped as his gaze alighted on the speaker.

"Are you going to stand there all night catching flies, or will you join us?" Blade asked.

Geronimo entered the car.

"Nice to see you again," Captain Stuart commented.

Blade pressed the button for the ground floor. "Where have you been?" he queried Geronimo as the door shut and the elevator began its descent.

"I took the shortcut."

"Here are some presents for you," Blade said, unslinging the SAR.

Geronimo leaned the AK-47 against the rear wall and took the Springfield, the Arminius, and the tomahawk. He hefted the latter and grinned. "I'm ready to go on the warpath now."

"What have you been doing? Goofing off?"

"I'll tell you all about it some year."

Blade stood next to the door and started reloading the Commando's magazine. "We'd be wiser taking the stairs, but we can't."

"Why not?" Geronimo inquired.

"My left leg is injured," Lyle disclosed. "There's no way I could handle twenty-five flights of stairs."

"This way is quicker," Blade commented. "But stay frosty

in case the elevator stops on the way down.''

"How about you?'' Geronimo questioned. ''Did you run into much trouble?''

"A few minor inconveniences.''

They fell silent, glued to the control panel, watching tensely as the numbers ticked off one by one. At the 11th floor the car commenced rocking back and forth.

"What's happening?'' Geronimo inquired in alarm.

Blade stared at the panel, waiting to hear a crash or a crunch and feel the elevator drop like a rock. If the grenades had damaged the shaft at the tenth floor, the car might fall or become wedged tightly. Neither prospect was appealing. He held his breath and saw the number ten light up, then the number nine.

The rocking ceased.

"What was that all about?'' Geronimo asked.

"Part of the tenth floor is missing,'' Blade explained.

"How'd that happen?''

"Faulty construction.''

The car lowered steadily until the elevator arrived and the door opened, revealing four Soviet soldiers, all of whom were clearly surprised at finding the car occupied. They gamely tried to bring their AK-47's into play.

Blade and Geronimo mowed the Russians down, the Commando and SAR perforating their torsos, slaying them before they could fire a single shot.

"Let's go,'' Blade said, walking over two of the bodies on his way to the front entrance.

"Dear Lord!'' Lyle exclaimed. ''I'm beginning to understand the reason only an idiot would mess with the Family.''

"Anyone who does answers to the Warriors,'' Blade stated.

"Which seems to be the equivalent of committing suicide,'' Lyle commented.

They walked to the junction and took a right, and spied the brown door at the end of the corridor.

"Is that the way out?'' Lyle queried.

"Yes,'' Blade told him. ''The Hurricane is in the parking

lot outside guarded by twelve soldiers.''

"I know," Lyle said. "I gave lessons to the six best Soviet pilots in the parking lot, but I was always brought down here blindfolded. The Butcher escorted me personally, and he would lead me all over the building before we ended up outside. I think he was trying to confuse me, to make me believe escape was impossible, that the Needle was a maze.''

"The Butcher will never confuse anyone again," Geronimo mentioned.

"You took care of him?" Blade asked.

"For all of us.''

"Too bad. I was hoping to introduce him to my Bowies.''

They were five feet from the door when Geronimo stopped abruptly and slapped his forehead. "Hold it!" he whispered.

Blade glanced at him. "What is it?"

"I remember the Butcher saying something about having two men guarding this door.''

"Is that so," Blade said, and handed the Commando to Captain Stuart. He stepped lightly to the door, drawing his Bowies, and used the tops of his fingers to twist the knob slowly and ease the door an inch from the jamb.

Sure enough, a pair of troopers were standing six feet from the doorway, craning their necks and gazing skyward.

How convenient, Blade thought, and came through the doorway in a rush, reaching the Russians in two leaps, swinging the Bowies up and in and imbedding the blades to the hilt, one in each guard's neck. He held on fast as their eyes widened and they dropped their AK-47's, their hands grasping at his wrists. Blood spurted over Blade's forearms as he shoved the troopers from him, tugging the knives out and sending the guards sprawling onto the asphalt.

"Here you go," Captain Stuart said, coming up on Blade's left and offering the Commando.

Blade wiped the Bowies on his pants and slid them into their sheaths. He glanced at the Hurricane as he took the Commando, and there were the 12 soldiers, all congregated near the tail of the VTOL, and every one was staring up at

Lenin's Needle. "Wha the—" he said, and looked in the same direction.

Bright red and orange flames were shooting from shattered windows on the tenth floor, and clouds of white smoke billowed from the crystal globe.

"What a beautiful sight," Lyle remarked.

"It's just the distraction we need," Blade stated, and raced toward the Hurricane, threading between the vehicles parked near the silver spire. He was 25 yards from the dozen troopers when he spotted a lone figure approaching them from the north. The newcomer's shirt was unbuttoned, his shirttail hanging out, and pearl-handled revolvers were visible at his waist.

"That's Hickok!" Geronimo exclaimed.

"What's he doing?" Lyle asked.

Blade saw the gunman halt not eight feet from the soldiers. Hickok spoke a few words to the Russians, but the distance was too great for Blade to hear what was said. The troopers whirled toward Nathan, and the gunfighter's hands were a streak as they pulled the Pythons. Six shots sounded almost as one, and six guards died with a slug through the head.

And then a strange thing happened.

Hickok held his fire, wagging his Colts at the remaining Russians, none of whom had their AK-47's unslung, and addressed them.

Blade was still 15 yards away. He was startled to see the guards slowly lowering their assault rifles to the ground. A moment later they were fleeing to the east as if a demon was on their tail.

"I don't believe it," Geronimo stated.

Hickok swung toward them, and a weary smile creased his face. "Howdy, pards. About time you got here."

"What was that all about?" Blade inquired, nodding at the departing Russians.

"I gave them a choice," Hickok said. "They figured they wanted to live."

Blade looked at Captain Stuart. "Fire up the Hurricane."

Lyle limped to the jet, to a rope ladder dangling from a door located under the cockpit. The Hurricanes were designed to ferry commando squads into combat, and the small access door enabled the strike force to drop or climb to the ground without exposing the pilot to enemy fire by raising the cockpit. Lyle clambered up the ladder.

Blade surveyed the parking lot, relieved to discover there wasn't a soldier in sight. The Russians in Lenin's Needle were undoubtedly in a total state of confusion, and additional troops had yet to arrive. He looked at Hickok, noting a peculiar, troubled aspect to his friend's expression. "Are you okay?"

Hickok sighed and started reloading his Pythons. "I'm gettin' a mite tired of all this killing."

Blade and Geronimo looked at one another.

"*You're* getting tired of killing?" Geronimo repeated in bewilderment.

"All we ever do is go around pluggin' cow-chips," Hickok said softly while ejecting a spent round from his right Colt. "The baddies attack us, and we attack them right back. They kill someone, and we kill them. There's always some varmint out to nail our hides to the wall, and we're always traipsing around the countryside teachin' them the error of their ways." He paused and sighed. "A lot of innocent folks have been killed along the way."

Geronimo placed his right hand on the gunman's left shoulder. "What's wrong? What's bothering you?"

"I don't know. I reckon I need a vacation real bad. Or maybe you've got the right idea. We've been doing this for years. Maybe we should retire, stop being Warriors, and spend more time with our families."

Blade and Geronimo were shocked, and their features showed as much.

"So if you're aimin' to quit, pard," Hickok said to Geronimo, "I'll hang up the Colts too."

Geronimo licked his lips and glanced at the silver spire, noting the flames were spreading. He stared into the gunman's eyes and squared his shoulders. "Uhhhh, I don't know how to tell you this."

"Tell me what?"

"I've changed my mind about quitting."

"You *what*?"

"I learned an important lesson on this run," Geronimo explained. "My quitting wouldn't make my wife and son any safer. They might sleep better at night, but I wouldn't. I'd know there was always someone out there scheming to destroy the Home and our Family. Let's face facts. Peace on earth and good will among all people will not come about until all the power-mongers and degenerates are eliminated. And as long as there's a need for Warriors to defend the Home and the Family, I intend to be one."

"You *changed* your mind," Hickok mumbled.

A tremendous roar shook the parking lot as the Hurricane's engine, a Rolls-Royce Pegasus Three turbofan that could supply 23,000 pounds of thrust, thundered to life.

"Into the VTOL," Blade shouted, dashing to the ladder and climbing into the cockpit. He took a seat behind Captain Stuart, who was wearing a flight helmet and inspecting the instrument panel. "Are we all set?"

Captain Stuart gave the thumb's-up sign with his right hand.

Geronimo and Hickok ascended the rope ladder, pulled it in after them, and closed the door. They took seats behind Blade, side by side. The cockpit was arranged with two rows of two seats apiece situated to the rear of the pilot, with a final solitary seat at the very back.

"Take it up," Blade ordered. "Do you have enough fuel to reach Denver?"

"There's fuel to spare."

"Good. Then you can drop us off near the SEAL and fly to Stapleton. President Toland and Governor Melnick will be glad to see you."

The VTOL began to rise slowly from the ground, using its vertical-takeoff capability to lift straight up.

Blade stared at the parking lot below, then at the spire.

"I should have known you'd change your blasted mind," Hickok declared.

"What's that crack supposed to mean?" Geronimo replied.

"You always were wishy-washy."

Captain Stuart banked the Hurricane and applied more thrust to the engine. The jet arced into the night sky, soaring high above Lenin's Needle.

"You know what to do," Blade stated.

Stuart nodded, winging the aircraft in a circle, and executed a tight dive, the nose angled at the silver spire. "Away she goes!" he cried, and a missile swooped toward its designated target. He pulled back on the stick and the Hurricane responded superbly, heading for the stars.

Blade shifted and gazed at the silver spire. The missile struck the edifice at about the 15th floor, and the resultant explosion blew out three whole stories as a billowing fireball enveloped the spire's midsection. Gravity took over, and the structure buckled and tilted, crumpling upon itself, and plunged toward the ground. Lenin's Needle, a monumental testimony to humanity's arrogance and passion for violence, crashed to the earth of its own pretentious weight.

"All right!" Captain Stuart declared happily.

Smiling, Blade settled back in his seat and relaxed, savoring the prospect of a peaceful flight to the SEAL and the return to the Home. But he should have known better.

"Hey, Lyle!" Hickok called out.

"What is it?"

"Does Geronimo's seat have an eject button?"